DREAM TALES AND PROSE POEMS

BY

IVAN TURGENEV

Translated from the Russian
by CONSTANCE GARNETT

faber and faber

This edition first published in 2008
by Faber and Faber Ltd
3 Queen Square, London WC1N 3AU

A CIP record for this book is available from the British Library

ISBN 978-0-571-24551-2

DREAM TALES AND PROSE POEMS

CONTENTS

CLARA MILITCH

CLARA MILITCH

I

In the spring of 1878 there was living in Moscow, in a small wooden house in Shabolovka, a young man of five-and-twenty, called Yakov Aratov. With him lived his father's sister, an elderly maiden lady, over fifty, Platonida Ivanovna. She took charge of his house, and looked after his household expenditure, a task for which Aratov was utterly unfit. Other relations he had none. A few years previously, his father, a provincial gentleman of small property, had moved to Moscow together with him and Platonida Ivanovna, whom he always, however, called Platosha; her nephew, too, used the same name. On leaving the country-place where they had always lived up till then, the elder Aratov settled in the old capital, with the object of putting his son to the university, for which he had himself prepared him; he bought for a trifle a little house in one of the outlying

3

streets, and established himself in it, with all his books and scientific odds and ends. And of books and odds and ends he had many — for he was a man of some considerable learning . . . 'an out-and-out eccentric,' as his neighbours said of him. He positively passed among them for a sorcerer; he had even been given the title of an 'insectivist.' He studied chemistry, mineralogy, entomology, botany, and medicine; he doctored patients gratis with herbs and metallic powders of his own invention, after the method of Paracelsus. These same powders were the means of his bringing to the grave his pretty, young, too delicate wife, whom he passionately loved, and by whom he had an only son. With the same powders he fairly ruined his son's health too, in the hope and intention of strengthening it, as he detected anaemia and a tendency to consumption in his constitution inherited from his mother. The name of 'sorcerer' had been given him partly because he regarded himself as a descendant—not in the direct line, of course—of the great Bruce, in honour of whom he had called his son Yakov, the Russian form of James.

He was what is called a most good-natured man, but of melancholy temperament, pottering, and timid, with a bent for everything mysterious and occult. . . . A half-whispered ah! was his habitual exclamation; he even died with this exclamation on his lips, two years after his removal to Moscow.

His son, Yakov, was in appearance unlike his father, who had been plain, clumsy, and awkward; he took more after his mother. He had the same delicate pretty features, the same soft ash-coloured hair, the same little aquiline nose, the same pouting childish lips, and great greenish-grey languishing eyes, with soft eyelashes. But in character he was like his father; and the face, so unlike the father's face, wore the father's expression; and he had the triangular-shaped hands and hollow chest of the old Aratov, who ought, however, hardly to be called old, since he never reached his fiftieth year. Before his death, Yakov had already entered the university in the faculty of physics and mathematics; he did not, however, complete his course; not through laziness, but because, according to his notions, you could learn no more in the university than you could studying alone at home; and he did not go in for a diploma because he had no idea of entering the government service. He was shy with his fellow-students, made friends with scarcely any one, especially held aloof from women, and lived in great solitude, buried in books. He

5

held aloof from women, though he had a heart of the tenderest, and was fascinated by beauty. . . . He had even obtained a sumptuous English keepsake, and (oh shame!) gloated adoringly over its 'elegantly engraved' representations of the various ravishing Gulnaras and Medoras. . . . But his innate modesty always kept him in check. In the house he used to work in what had been his father's study, it was also his bedroom, and his bed was the very one in which his father had breathed his last.

The mainstay of his whole existence, his unfailing friend and companion, was his aunt Platosha, with whom he exchanged barely a dozen words in the day, but without whom he could not stir hand or foot. She was a long-faced, long-toothed creature, with pale eyes, and a pale face, with an invariable expression, half of dejection, half of anxious dismay. For ever garbed in a grey dress and a grey shawl, she wandered about the house like a spirit, with noiseless steps, sighed, murmured prayers— especially one favourite one, consisting of three words only, 'Lord, succour us!'—and looked after the house with much good sense, taking care of every halfpenny, and buying everything herself. Her nephew she adored; she was in a perpetual fidget over his health—afraid of

6

everything—not for herself but for him; and directly she fancied the slightest thing wrong, she would steal in softly, and set a cup of herb tea on his writing-table, or stroke him on the spine with her hands, soft as wadding. Yakov was not annoyed by these attentions—though the herb tea he left untouched—he merely nodded his head approvingly. However, his health was really nothing to boast of. He was very impressionable, nervous, fanciful, suffered from palpitations of the heart, and sometimes from asthma; like his father, he believed that there are in nature and in the soul of man, mysteries which may sometimes be divined, but to which one can never penetrate; he believed in the existence of certain powers and influences, sometimes beneficent, but more often malignant, . . . and he believed too in science, in its dignity and importance. Of late he had taken a great fancy to photography. The smell of the chemicals used in this pursuit was a source of great uneasiness to his old aunt—not on her own account again, but on Yasha's, on account of his chest; but for all the softness of his temper, there was not a little obstinacy in his composition, and he persisted in his favourite pursuit. Platosha gave in, and only sighed more than ever, and murmured, 'Lord, succour us!' whenever she saw his fingers stained with iodine.

7

Yakov, as we have already related, had held aloof from his fellow-students; with one of them he had, however, become fairly intimate, and saw him frequently, even after the fellow-student had left the university and entered the service, in a position involving little responsibility. He had, in his own words, got on to the building of the Church of our Saviour, though, of course, he knew nothing whatever of architecture. Strange to say, this one solitary friend of Aratov's, by name Kupfer, a German, so far Russianised that he did not know one word of German, and even fell foul of 'the Germans,' this friend had apparently nothing in common with him. He was a black-haired, red-cheeked young man, very jovial, talkative, and devoted to the feminine society Aratov so assiduously avoided. It is true Kupfer both lunched and dined with him pretty often, and even, being a man of small means, used to borrow trifling sums of him; but this was not what induced the free and easy German to frequent the humble little house in Shabolovka so diligently. The spiritual purity, the idealism of Yakov pleased him, possibly as a contrast to what he was seeing and meeting every day; or possibly this very attachment to the youthful idealist betrayed him of German blood after all. Yakov liked Kupfer's simple-hearted frankness;

8

and besides that, his accounts of the theatres, concerts, and balls, where he was always in attendance—of the unknown world altogether, into which Yakov could not make up his mind to enter—secretly interested and even excited the young hermit, without, however, arousing any desire to learn all this by his own experience. And Platosha made Kupfer welcome; it is true she thought him at times excessively unceremonious, but instinctively perceiving and realising that he was sincerely attached to her precious Yasha, she not only put up with the noisy guest, but felt kindly towards him.

II

At the time with which our story is concerned, there was in Moscow a certain widow, a Georgian princess, a person of somewhat dubious, almost suspicious character. She was close upon forty; in her youth she had probably bloomed with that peculiar Oriental beauty, which fades so quickly; now she powdered, rouged, and dyed her hair yellow. Various reports, not altogether favourable, nor altogether definite, were in circulation about her; her husband no one had known, and she had never stayed long in any one town. She had no children, and no property, yet she kept open house, in debt or otherwise; she had a salon, as it is called, and received a rather mixed society, for the most part young men. Everything in her house from her own dress, furniture, and table, down to her carriage and her servants, bore the stamp of something shoddy, artificial, temporary, . . . but the princess herself, as well as her guests, apparently desired nothing better. The princess was reputed a devotee of music and literature, a patroness of artists and men of talent, and she really was interested in all these subjects, even to the point of enthusiasm, and an enthusiasm not altogether affected. There was an unmistakable fibre of artistic feeling in her. Moreover she was very approachable, genial, free from presumption or pretentiousness, and, though many people did not suspect it, she was fundamentally good-natured, soft-hearted, and kindly disposed. . . . Qualities rare—and the more precious for their rarity—precisely in persons of her sort! 'A fool of a woman!' a wit said of her: 'but she'll get into heaven, not a doubt of it! Because she forgives everything, and everything will be forgiven her.' It was said of her too that when she disappeared from a town, she always left as many creditors behind as persons she had befriended. A soft heart readily turned in any direction.

Kupfer, as might have been anticipated, found his way into her house, and was soon on an intimate—evil tongues said a too intimate—footing with her. He himself always spoke of her not only affectionately but with respect; he called her a heart of gold—say what you like! and firmly believed both in her love for art and her comprehension of art! One day after dinner at the Aratovs', in discussing the princess and her evenings, he began to persuade Yakov to break for once from his anchorite seclusion, and to allow him, Kupfer, to present him to his friend. Yakov at first would not even hear of it 'But what do you imagine?' Kupfer cried at last: 'what sort of presentation are we talking about? Simply, I take you, just as you are sitting now, in your everyday coat, and go with you to her for an evening. No sort of etiquette is necessary there, my dear boy! You're learned, you know, and fond of literature and music'—(there actually was in Aratov's study a piano on which he sometimes struck minor chords)—'and in her house there's enough and to spare of all those goods! . . . and you'll meet there sympathetic people, no nonsense about them! And after all, you really can't at your age, with your looks

(Aratov dropped his eyes and waved his hand deprecatingly), yes, yes, with your looks, you really can't keep aloof from society, from the world, like this! Why, I'm not going to take you to see generals! Indeed, I know no generals myself! . . . Don't be obstinate, dear boy! Morality is an excellent thing, most laudable. . . . But why fall a prey to asceticism? You're not going in for becoming a monk!'

Aratov was, however, still refractory; but Kupfer found an unexpected ally in Platonida Ivanovna. Though she had no clear idea what was meant by the word asceticism, she too was of opinion that it would be no harm for dear Yasha to take a little recreation, to see people, and to show himself.

'Especially,' she added, 'as I've perfect confidence in Fyodor Fedoritch! He'll take you to no bad place! . . .' 'I'll bring him back in all his maiden innocence,' shouted Kupfer, at which Platonida Ivanovna, in spite of her confidence, cast uneasy glances upon him. Aratov blushed up to his ears, but ceased to make objections.

It ended by Kupfer taking him next day to spend an evening at the princess's. But Aratov did not remain there long. To begin with, he found there some twenty visitors, men

and women, sympathetic people possibly, but
still strangers, and this oppressed him, even
though he had to do very little talking; and
that, he feared above all things. Secondly, he
did not like their hostess, though she received
him very graciously and simply. Everything
about her was distasteful to him: her painted
face, and her frizzed curls, and her thickly-
sugary voice, her shrill giggle, her way of
rolling her eyes and looking up, her excessively low-necked dress, and those fat, glossy
fingers with their multitude of rings! . . .
Hiding himself away in a corner, he took from
time to time a rapid survey of the faces of all
the guests, without even distinguishing them,
and then stared obstinately at his own feet.
When at last a stray musician with a worn
face, long hair, and an eyeglass stuck into his
contorted eyebrow sat down to the grand piano
and flinging his hands with a sweep on the keys
and his foot on the pedal, began to attack a
fantasia of Liszt on a Wagner motive, Aratov
could not stand it, and stole off, bearing away
in his heart a vague, painful impression; across
which, however, flitted something incomprehensible to him, but grave and even disquieting.

III

KUPFER came next day to dinner; he did not begin, however, expatiating on the preceding evening, he did not even reproach Aratov for his hasty retreat, and only regretted that he had not stayed to supper, when there had been champagne! (of the Novgorod brand, we may remark in parenthesis). Kupfer probably realised that it had been a mistake on his part to disturb his friend, and that Aratov really was a man 'not suited' to that circle and way of life. On his side, too, Aratov said nothing of the princess, nor of the previous evening. Platonida Ivanovna did not know whether to rejoice at the failure of this first experiment or to regret it. She decided at last that Yasha's health might suffer from such outings, and was comforted. Kupfer went away directly after dinner, and did not show himself again for a whole week. And it was not that he resented the failure of his suggestion, the good fellow was incapable of that, but he had obviously found some interest which was absorbing all his time, all his thoughts; for later on, too, he rarely appeared at the Aratovs', had an absorbed look, spoke little and quickly vanished. . . . Aratov went on living as before; but a sort of—if one may so express it—little hook was pricking at his soul. He was continually haunted by some reminiscence, he could not quite tell what it was himself, and this reminiscence was connected with the evening he had spent at the princess's. For all that he had not the slightest inclination to return there again, and the world, a part of which he had looked upon at her house, repelled him more than ever. So passed six weeks.

And behold one morning Kupfer stood before him once more, this time with a somewhat embarrassed countenance. 'I know,' he began with a constrained smile, 'that your visit that time was not much to your taste; but I hope for all that you'll agree to my proposal . . that you won't refuse me my request!'

'What is it?' inquired Aratov.

'Well, do you see,' pursued Kupfer, getting more and more heated: 'there is a society here of amateurs, artistic people, who from time to time get up readings, concerts, even theatrical performances for some charitable object.'

'And the princess has a hand in it?' interposed Aratov.

'The princess has a hand in all good deeds, but That's not the point. We have arranged a literary and musical matinée . . . and at this

matinée you may hear a girl . . . an extraordinary girl! We cannot make out quite yet
whether she is to be a Rachel or a Viardot . . .
for she sings exquisitely, and recites and plays.
. . . A talent of the very first rank, my dear
boy! I'm not exaggerating. Well then, won't
you take a ticket? Five roubles for a seat in
the front row.'

'And where has this marvellous girl sprung
from?' asked Aratov.

Kupfer grinned. 'That I really can't say.
. . . Of late she's found a home with the
princess. The princess you know is a protector
of every one of that sort. . . . But you saw her,
most likely, that evening.'

Aratov gave a faint inward start . . . but he
said nothing.

'She has even played somewhere in the provinces,' Kupfer continued, 'and altogether she's
created for the theatre. There! you'll see for
yourself!'

'What's her name?' asked Aratov.

'Clara . . .'

'Clara?' Aratov interrupted a second time.
'Impossible!'

'Why impossible? Clara . . . Clara Militch;
it's not her real name . . . but that's what she's
called. She's going to sing a song of Glinka's
. . . and of Tchaykovsky's; and then she'll

recite the letter from *Yevgeny Oniegin*. Well; will you take a ticket?'

'And when will it be?'

'To-morrow . . . to-morrow, at half-past one, in a private drawing-room, in Ostozhonka. . . . I will come for you. A five-rouble ticket? . . . Here it is . . . no, that's a three-rouble one. Here . . . and here's the programme. . . . I'm one of the stewards.'

Aratov sank into thought Platonida Ivanovna came in at that instant, and glancing at his face, was in a flutter of agitation at once. 'Yasha,' she cried, 'what's the matter with you? Why are you so upset? Fyodor Fedoritch, what is it you've been telling him?'

Aratov did not let his friend answer his aunt's question, but hurriedly snatching the ticket held out to him, told Platonida Ivanovna to give Kupfer five roubles at once.

She blinked in amazement. . . . However, she handed Kupfer the money in silence. Her darling Yasha had ejaculated his commands in a very imperative manner.

'I tell you, a wonder of wonders!' cried Kupfer, hurrying to the door. 'Wait till to-morrow.'

'Has she black eyes?' Aratov called after him.

'Black as coal!' Kupfer shouted cheerily, as he vanished.

Aratov went away to his room, while Platonida Ivanovna stood rooted to the spot, repeating in a whisper, 'Lord, succour us I Succour
us, Lord!'

IV

THE big drawing-room in the private house in
Ostozhonka was already half full of visitors when
Aratov and Kupfer arrived. Dramatic performances had sometimes been given in this drawing-room, but on this occasion there was no
scenery nor curtain visible. The organisers
of the matinée had confined themselves to
fixing up a platform at one end, putting upon
it a piano, a couple of reading-desks, a few
chairs, a table with a bottle of water and a glass
on it, and hanging red cloth over the door that
led to the room allotted to the performers. In
the first row was already sitting the princess in
a bright green dress. Aratov placed himself at
some distance from her, after exchanging the
barest of greetings with her. The public was,
as they say, of mixed materials; for the most
part young men from educational institutions.
Kupfer, as one of the stewards, with a white
ribbon on the cuff of his coat, fussed and

bustled about busily; the princess was obviously excited, looked about her, shot smiles in all directions, talked with those next her . . . none but men were sitting near her. The first to appear on the platform was a flute-player of consumptive appearance, who most conscientiously dribbled away—what am I saying?—piped, I mean—a piece also of consumptive tendency; two persons shouted bravo! Then a stout gentleman in spectacles, of an exceedingly solid, even surly aspect, read in a bass voice a sketch of Shtchedrin; the sketch was applauded, not the reader; then the pianist, whom Aratov had seen before, came forward and strummed the same fantasia of Liszt; the pianist gained an encore. He bowed with one hand on the back of the chair, and after each bow he shook back his hair, precisely like Liszt! At last after a rather long interval the red cloth over the door on to the platform stirred and opened wide, and Clara Militch appeared. The room resounded with applause. With hesitating steps, she moved forward on the platform, stopped and stood motionless, clasping her large handsome ungloved hands in front of her, without a courtesy, a bend of the head, or a smile.

She was a girl of nineteen, tall, rather broad-shouldered, but well-built. A dark face, of a half-Jewish half-gipsy type, small black eyes under thick brows almost meeting in the middle, a straight, slightly turned-up nose, delicate lips with a beautiful but decided curve, an immense mass of black hair, heavy even in appearance, a low brow still as marble, tiny ears . . . the whole face dreamy, almost sullen. A nature passionate, wilful—hardly good-tempered, hardly very clever, but gifted—was expressed in every feature.

For some time she did not raise her eyes; but suddenly she started, and passed over the rows of spectators a glance intent, but not attentive, absorbed, it seemed, in herself. . . . 'What tragic eyes she has!' observed a man sitting behind Aratov, a grey-headed dandy with the face of a Revel harlot, well known in Moscow as a prying gossip and writer for the papers. The dandy was an idiot, and meant to say something idiotic . . . but he spoke the truth. Aratov, who from the very moment of Clara's entrance had never taken his eyes off her, only at that instant recollected that he really had seen her at the princess's; and not only that he had seen her, but that he had even noticed that she had several times, with a peculiar insistency, gazed at him with her dark intent eyes. And now too—or was it his fancy?—on seeing him in the front row she seemed delighted, seemed to flush, and again gazed intently at him. Then, without turning round, she stepped away a couple of paces in the direction of the piano, at which her accompanist, a long-haired foreigner, was sitting. She had to render Glinka's ballad: 'As soon as I knew you . . .' She began at once to sing, without changing the attitude of her hands or glancing at the music. Her voice was soft and resonant, a contralto; she uttered the words distinctly and with emphasis, and sang monotonously, with little light and shade, but with intense expression. 'The girl sings with conviction,' said the same dandy sitting behind Aratov, and again he spoke the truth. Shouts of 'Bis!' 'Bravo!' resounded over the room; but she flung a rapid glance on Aratov, who neither shouted nor clapped—he did not particularly care for her singing—gave a slight bow, and walked out without taking the hooked arm proffered her by the long-haired pianist. She was called back . . . not very soon, she reappeared, with the same hesitating steps approached the piano, and whispering a couple of words to the accompanist, who picked out and put before him another piece of music, began Tchaykovsky's song: 'No, only he who knows the thirst to see.' . . . This song she sang differently from the first—in a low voice, as though she were tired . . . and only at the line next the last, 'He knows what I have suffered,' broke from her in a ringing, passionate cry. The last line, 'And how I suffer' . . . she almost whispered, with a mournful prolongation of the last word. This song produced less impression on the audience than the Glinka ballad; there was much applause, however. . . . Kupfer was particularly conspicuous; folding his hands in a peculiar way, in the shape of a barrel, at each clap he produced an extraordinarily resounding report. The princess handed him a large, straggling nosegay for him to take it to the singer; but she, seeming not to observe Kupfer's bowing figure, and outstretched hand with the nosegay, turned and went away, again without waiting for the pianist, who skipped forward to escort her more hurriedly than before, and when he found himself so unjustifiably deserted, tossed his hair as certainly Liszt himself had never tossed his!

During the whole time of the singing, Aratov had been watching Clara's face. It seemed to him that her eyes, through the drooping eyelashes, were again turned upon him; but he was especially struck by the immobility of the face, the forehead, the eyebrows; and only at her outburst of passion he caught through the hardly-parted lips the warm gleam of a close row of white teeth. Kupfer came up to him.

'Well, my dear boy, what do you think of her?' he asked, beaming all over with satisfaction.

'It's a fine voice,' replied Aratov; 'but she doesn't know how to sing yet; she 's no real musical knowledge.' (Why he said this, and what conception he had himself of 'musical knowledge,' the Lord only knows!)

Kupfer was surprised. 'No musical knowledge,' he repeated slowly. . . . 'Well, as to that . . . she can acquire that. But what soul! Wait a bit, though; you shall hear her in Tatiana's letter.'

He hurried away from Aratov, while the latter said to himself, 'Soul! with that immovable face!' He thought that she moved and held herself like one hypnotised, like a somnambulist. And at the same time she was unmistakably . . . yes! unmistakably looking at him.

Meanwhile the matinée went on. The fat man in spectacles appeared again; in spite of his serious exterior, he fancied himself a comic actor, and recited a scene from Gogol, this time without eliciting a single token of approbation. There was another glimpse of the flute-player; another thunder-clap from the pianist; a boy of twelve, frizzed and pomaded, but with tear-stains on his cheeks, thrummed some variations on a riddle. What seemed strange was that in the intervals of the reading and music, from the performers' room, sounds were heard from time to time of a French horn; and yet this instrument never was brought into requisition. In the sequel it appeared that the amateur, who had been invited to perform on it, had lost courage at the moment of facing the public. At last Clara Militch made her appearance again.

She held a volume of Pushkin in her hand; she did not, however, glance at it once during her recitation. . . . She was obviously nervous, the little book shook slightly in her ringers. Aratov observed also the expression of weariness which now overspread all her stern features. The first line, 'I write to you . . . what more?' she uttered exceedingly simply, almost naïvely, and with a naïve, genuine, helpless gesture held both hands out before her. Then she began to hurry a little; but from the beginning of the lines: 'Another! no! To no one in the whole world I have given my heart!' she mastered her powers, gained fire; and when she came to the words, 'My whole life has but been a pledge of a meeting true with thee,' her hitherto thick voice rang out boldly and enthusiastically,

while her eyes just as boldly and directly
fastened upon Aratov. She went on with the
same fervour, and only towards the end her
voice dropped again; and in it, and in her face,
the same weariness was reflected again. The
last four lines she completely 'murdered,' as it
is called; the volume of Pushkin suddenly slid
out of her hand, and she hastily withdrew.

The audience fell to applauding desperately,
encoring. . . . One Little-Russian divinity stu-
dent bellowed in so deep a bass, 'Mill-itch!
Mill-itch!' that his neighbour civilly and sym-
pathetically advised him, 'to take care of his
voice, it would be the making of a protodeacon.'
But Aratov at once rose and made for the
door. Kupfer overtook him. . . . 'I say, where
are you off to?' he called; 'would you like
me to present you to Clara?' 'No, thanks,'
Aratov returned hurriedly, and he went homewards almost at a run.

V

HE was agitated by strange sensations, incomprehensible to himself. In reality, Clara's
recitation, too, had not been quite to his taste
. . . though he could not quite tell why. It

disturbed him, this recitation; it struck him as crude and inharmonious. . . . It was as though it broke something within him, forced itself with a certain violence upon him. And those fixed, insistent, almost importunate looks— what were they for? what did they mean?

Aratov's modesty did not for one instant admit of the idea that he might have made an impression on this strange girl, that he might have inspired in her a sentiment akin to love, to passion! . . . And indeed, he himself had formed a totally different conception of the still unknown woman, the girl to whom he was to give himself wholly, who would love him, be his bride, his wife. . . . He seldom dwelt on this dream — in spirit as in body he was virginal; but the pure image that arose at such times in his fancy was inspired by a very different figure, the figure of his dead mother, whom he scarcely remembered, but whose portrait he treasured as a sacred relic. The portrait was a water-colour, painted rather un-skilfully by a lady who had been a neighbour of hers; but the likeness, as every one declared, was a striking one. Just such a tender profile, just such kind, clear eyes and silken hair, just such a smile and pure expression, was the woman, the girl, to have, for whom as yet he scarcely dared to hope. . . .

But this swarthy, dark-skinned creature, with coarse hair, dark eyebrows, and a tiny moustache on her upper lip, she was certainly a wicked, giddy . . . 'gipsy' (Aratov could not imagine a harsher appellation)—what was she to him?

And yet Aratov could not succeed in getting out of his head this dark-skinned gipsy, whose singing and reading and very appearance were displeasing to him. He was puzzled, he was angry with himself. Not long before he had read Sir Walter Scott's novel, *St. Ronan's Well* (there was a complete edition of Sir Walter Scott's works in the library of his father, who had regarded the English novelist with esteem as a serious, almost a scientific, writer). The heroine of that novel is called Clara Mowbray. A poet who flourished somewhere about 1840, Krasov, wrote a poem on her, ending with the words:

> 'Unhappy Clara! poor frantic Clara!
> Unhappy Clara Mowbray!'

Aratov knew this poem also. . . . And now these words were incessantly haunting his memory. . . . 'Unhappy Clara! Poor, frantic Clara!' . . . (This was why he had been so surprised when Kupfer told him the name of Clara Militch.)

Platosha herself noticed, not a change exactly in Yasha's temper—no change in reality took place in it—but something unsatisfactory in his looks and in his words. She cautiously questioned him about the literary matinée at which he had been present; muttered, sighed, looked at him from in front, from the side, from behind; and suddenly clapping her hands on her thighs, she exclaimed: 'To be sure, Yasha; I see what it is!'

'Why? what?' Aratov queried.

'You've met for certain at that matinée one of those long-tailed creatures'—this was how Platonida Ivanovna always spoke of all fashion-ably-dressed ladies of the period—'with a pretty dolly face; and she goes prinking *this* way . . . and pluming *that* way'—Platonida presented these fancied manœuvres in mimicry —'and making saucers like this with her eyes' —and she drew big, round circles in the air with her forefinger—'You're not used to that sort of thing. So you fancied . . . but that means nothing, Yasha . . . no-o-thing at all! Drink a cup of posset at night . . . it'll pass off! . . . Lord, succour us!'

Platosha ceased speaking, and left the room. . . . She had hardly ever uttered such a long and animated speech in her life. . . . While Aratov thought, 'Auntie's right, I dare say. . . . I'm not used to it; that's all . . . '—it actually was the first time his attention had ever happened to be drawn to a person of the female sex . . . at least he had never noticed it before— 'I mustn't give way to it.'

And he set to work on his books, and at night drank some lime-flower tea; and positively slept well that night, and had no dreams. The next morning he took up his photography again as though nothing had happened. . . .

But towards evening his spiritual repose was again disturbed.

VI

AND this is what happened. A messenger brought him a note, written in a large irregular woman's hand, and containing the following lines:

'If you guess who it is writes to you, and if it is not a bore to you, come to-morrow after dinner to the Tversky boulevard—about five o'clock—and wait. You shall not be kept long. But it is very important. Do come.'

There was no signature. Aratov at once guessed who was his correspondent, and this was just what disturbed him. 'What folly,' he said, almost aloud; 'this is too much. Of course I shan't go.' He sent, however, for the messenger, and from him learnt nothing but that the note had been handed him by a maid-servant in the street. Dismissing him, Aratov read the letter through and flung it on the ground. . . . But, after a little while, he picked it up and read it again: a second time he cried, 'Folly!'—he did not, however, throw the note on the floor again, but put it in a drawer. Aratov took up his ordinary occupations, first one and then another; but nothing he did was success-ful or satisfactory. He suddenly realised that he was eagerly expecting Kupfer! Did he want to question him, or perhaps even to con-fide in him? . . . But Kupfer did not make his appearance. Then Aratov took down Pushkin, read Tatiana's letter, and convinced himself again that the 'gipsy girl' had not in the least understood the real force of the letter. And that donkey Kupfer shouts: Rachel! Viardot! Then he went to his piano, as it seemed, uncon-sciously opened it, and tried to pick out by ear the melody of Tchaykovsky's song; but he slammed it to again directly in vexation, and went up to his aunt to her special room, which was for ever baking hot, smelled of mint, sage, and other medicinal herbs, and was littered up with such a multitude of rugs, side-tables, stools, cushions, and padded furniture of all sorts, that any one unused to it would have found it difficult to turn round and oppressive to breathe in it Platonida Ivanovna was sitting at the window, her knitting in her hands (she was knitting her darling Yasha a comforter, the thirty-eighth she had made him in the course of his life!), and was much astonished to see him. Aratov rarely went up to her, and if he wanted anything, used always to call, in his delicate voice, from his study: 'Aunt Platosha!' However, she made him sit down, and sat all alert, in expectation of his first words, watching him through her spectacles with one eye, over them with the other. She did not inquire after his health nor offer him tea, as she saw he had not come for that. Aratov was a little disconcerted . . . then he began to talk . . . talked of his mother, of how she had lived with his father and how his father had got to know her. All this he knew very well . . . but it was just what he wanted to talk about Unluckily for him, Platosha did not know how to keep up a conversation at all; she gave him very brief replies, as though she suspected that was not what Yasha had come for.

'Eh!' she repeated, hurriedly, almost irritably plying her knitting-needles. 'We all know: your mother was a darling . . . a darling that she was. . . . And your father loved her as a husband should, truly and faithfully even in her grave; and he never loved any other woman': she added, raising her voice and taking off her spectacles.

'And was she of a retiring disposition?' Aratov inquired, after a short silence.

'Retiring! to be sure she was. As a woman should be. Bold ones have sprung up nowadays.'

'And were there no bold ones in your time?'

'There were in our time too . . . to be sure there were! But who were they? A pack of strumpets, shameless hussies. Draggle-tails— for ever gadding about after no good. . . . What do they care? It's little they take to heart. If some poor fool comes in their way, they pounce on him. But sensible folk looked down on them. Did you ever see, pray, the like of such in our house?'

Aratov made no reply, and went back to his study. Platonida Ivanovna looked after him, shook her head, put on her spectacles again, and again took up her comforter . . . but more than once sank into thought, and let her knitting-needles fall on her knees.

Aratov up till very night kept telling himself, no! no! but with the same irritation, the same exasperation, he fell again into musing on the note, on the 'gipsy girl,' on the appointed meeting, to which he would certainly not go!

And at night she gave him no rest. He was continually haunted by her eyes—at one time half-closed, at another wide open—and their persistent gaze fixed straight upon him, and those motionless features with their dominating expression. . . .

The next morning he again, for some reason, kept expecting Kupfer; he was on the point of writing a note to him . . . but did nothing, however, . . . and spent most of the time walking up and down his room. He never for one instant admitted to himself even the idea of going to this idiotic rendezvous . . . and at half-past three, after a hastily swallowed dinner, suddenly throwing on his cloak and thrusting his cap on his head, he dashed out into the street, unseen by his aunt, and turned towards the Tversky boulevard.

VII

ARATOV found few people walking in it. The weather was damp and rather cold. He tried not to reflect on what he was doing, to force himself to turn his attention to every object that presented itself, and, as it were, persuaded himself that he had simply come out for a walk

like the other people passing to and fro. . . .
The letter of the day before was in his breast-
pocket, and he was conscious all the while of
its presence there. He walked twice up and
down the boulevard, scrutinised sharply every
feminine figure that came near him—and his
heart throbbed. . . . He felt tired and sat
down on a bench. And suddenly the thought
struck him: 'What if that letter was not written
by her, but to some one else by some other
woman?' In reality this should have been a
matter of indifference to him . . . and yet he
had to admit to himself that he did not want
this to be so. 'That would be too silly,' he
thought, 'even sillier than *this*!' A nervous
unrest began to gain possession of him; he
began to shiver—not outwardly, but inwardly.
He several times took his watch out of his
waistcoat pocket, looked at the face, put it back,
and each time forgot how many minutes it was
to five. He fancied that every passer-by looked
at him in a peculiar way, with a sort of sarcastic
astonishment and curiosity. A wretched little
dog ran up, sniffed at his legs, and began
wagging its tail. He threatened it angrily.
He was particularly annoyed by a factory lad
in a greasy smock, who seated himself on a
seat on the other side of the boulevard, and
by turns whistling, scratching himself, and

34

swinging his feet in enormous tattered boots, persistently stared at him. 'And his master,' thought Aratov, 'is waiting for him, no doubt, while he, lazy scamp, is kicking up his heels here. . . .'

But at that very instant he felt that some one had come up and was standing close behind him . . . there was a breath of something warm from behind. . . .

He looked round. . . . She!

He knew her at once, though a thick, dark blue veil hid her features. He instantaneously leapt up from the seat, but stopped short, and could not utter a word. She too was silent. He felt great embarrassment; but her embarrassment was no less. Aratov, even through the veil, could not help noticing how deadly pale she had turned. Yet she was the first to speak.

'Thanks,' she began in an unsteady voice, 'thanks for coming. I did not expect . . .' She turned a little away and walked along the boulevard. Aratov walked after her.

'You have, perhaps, thought ill of me,' she went on, without turning her head; 'indeed, my conduct is very strange. . . . But I had heard so much about you . . . but no! I . . . that was not the reason. . . . If only you knew . . . There was so much I wanted to tell you,

35

my God! . . . But how to do it . . . how to do it!'

Aratov was walking by her side, a little behind her; he could not see her face; he saw only her hat and part of her veil . . . and her long black shabby cape. All his irritation, both with her and with himself, suddenly came back to him; all the absurdity, the awkwardness of this interview, these explanations between perfect strangers in a public promenade, suddenly struck him.

'I have come on your invitation,' he began in his turn. 'I have come, my dear madam' (her shoulders gave a faint twitch, she turned off into a side passage, he followed her), 'simply to clear up, to discover to what strange misunderstanding it is due that you are pleased to address me, a stranger to you . . . who . . . only *guessed*, to use your expression in your letter, that it was you writing to him... guessed it because during that literary matinée, you saw fit to pay him such . . . such obvious attention.'

All this little speech was delivered by Aratov in that ringing but unsteady voice in which very young people answer at examinations on a subject in which they are well prepared. . . . He was angry; he was furious. . . . It was just this fury which loosened his ordinarily not very ready tongue.

She still went on along the walk with rather slower steps. . . . Aratov, as before, walked after her, and as before saw only the old cape and the hat, also not a very new one. His vanity suffered at the idea that she must now be thinking: 'I had only to make a sign —and he rushed at once!'

Aratov was silent . . . he expected her to answer him; but she did not utter a word.

'I am ready to listen to you,' he began again, 'and shall be very glad if I can be of use to you in any way . . . though I am, I confess, surprised . . . considering the retired life I lead. . . .'

At these last words of his, Clara suddenly turned to him, and he beheld such a terrified, such a deeply-wounded face, with such large bright tears in the eyes, such a pained expression about the parted lips, and this face was so lovely, that he involuntarily faltered, and himself felt something akin to terror and pity and softening.

'Ah, why . . . why are you like that?' she said, with an irresistibly genuine and truthful force, and how movingly her voice rang out! 'Could my turning to you be offensive to you? . . . is it possible you have understood nothing? . . . Ah, yes! you have understood nothing, you did not understand what I said to you,

37

God knows what you have been imagining about me, you have not even dreamed what it cost me—to write to you! . . . You thought of nothing but yourself, your own dignity, your peace of mind! . . . But is it likely I' . . . (she squeezed her hands raised to her lips so hard, that the fingers gave a distinct crack). . . . 'As though I made any sort of demands of you, as though explanations were necessary first. . . . "My dear madam, . . . I am, I confess, surprised, . . . if I can be of any use" . . . Ah! I am mad!—I was mistaken in you—in your face! . . . when I saw you the first time. . .! Here . . . you stand. . . . If only one word. What, not one word?'

She ceased. . . . Her face suddenly flushed, and as suddenly took a wrathful and insolent expression. 'Mercy! how idiotic this is!' she cried suddenly, with a shrill laugh. 'How idiotic our meeting is! What a fool I am! . . . and you too. . . . Ugh!'

She gave a contemptuous wave of her hand, as though motioning him out of her road, and passing him, ran quickly out of the boulevard, and vanished.

The gesture of her hand, the insulting laugh, and the last exclamation, at once carried Aratov back to his first frame of mind, and stifled the feeling that had sprung up in his heart when she turned to him with tears in her eyes. He was angry again, and almost shouted after the retreating girl: 'You may make a good actress, but why did you think fit to play off this farce on me?'

He returned home with long strides, and though he still felt anger and indignation all the way, yet across these evil, malignant feelings, unconsciously, the memory forced itself of the exquisite face he had seen for a single moment only. . . . He even put himself the question, 'Why did I not answer her when she asked of me only a word? I had not time,' he thought. 'She did not let me utter the word . . . and what word could I have uttered?'

But he shook his head at once, and murmured reproachfully, 'Actress!'

And again, at the same time, the vanity of the inexperienced nervous youth, at first wounded, was now, as it were, flattered at having any way inspired such a passion. . . .

'Though by now,' he pursued his reflections, 'it's all over, of course. . . . I must have seemed absurd to her.' . . .

This idea was disagreeable to him, and again he was angry . . . both with her . . . and with himself. On reaching home, he shut himself up in his study. He did not want to see Platosha.

The good old lady came twice to his locked door, put her ear to the keyhole, and only sighed and murmured her prayer.

'It has begun!' she thought. . . . 'And he only five-and-twenty! Ah, it's early, it's early!'

VIII

ALL the following day Aratov was in very low spirits. 'What is it, Yasha?' Platonida Ivanovna said to him: 'you seem somehow all loose ends to-day!' . . . In her own peculiar idiom the old lady's expression described fairly accurately Aratov's mental condition. He could not work and he did not know himself what he wanted. At one time he was eagerly on the watch for Kupfer, again he suspected that it was from Kupfer that Clara had got his address . . . and from where else could she 'have heard so much about him'? Then he wondered: was it possible his acquaintance with her was to end like this? Then he fancied she would write to him again; then he asked himself whether he ought not to write her a letter, explaining everything, since he did not at all like leaving an unfavourable impression of himself. . . . But exactly what to explain? Then he stirred up in himself almost a feeling of repulsion for her, for her insistence, her impertinence; and then again he saw that unutterably touching face and heard an irresistible voice; then he recalled her singing, her recitation— and could not be sure whether he had been right in his wholesale condemnation of it. In fact, he was all loose ends! At last he was heartily sick of it, and resolved to keep a firm hand over himself, as it is called, and to obliterate the whole incident, as it was unmistakably hindering his studies and destroying his peace of mind. It turned out not so easy to carry out this resolution . . . more than a week passed by before he got back into his old accustomed groove. Luckily Kupfer did not turn up at all; he was in fact out of Moscow. Not long before the incident, Aratov had begun to work at painting in connection with his photographic plans; he set to work upon it now with redoubled zest.

So, imperceptibly, with a few (to use the doctors' expression) 'symptoms of relapse,' manifested, for instance, in his once almost deciding to call upon the princess, two months passed . . . then three months . . . and Aratov was the old Aratov again. Only somewhere down below, under the surface of his life, something like a dark and burdensome secret dogged him wherever he went. So a great fish just caught on the hook, but not yet drawn up, will swim at the bottom of a deep stream under the very boat where the angler sits with a stout rod in his hand.

And one day, skimming through a not quite new number of the *Moscow Gazette*, Aratov lighted upon the following paragraph:

'With the greatest regret,' wrote some local contributor from Kazan, 'we must add to our dramatic record the news of the sudden death of our gifted actress Clara Militch, who had succeeded during the brief period of her engagement in becoming a favourite of our discriminating public. Our regret is the more poignant from the fact that Miss Militch by her own act cut short her young life, so full of promise, by means of poison. And this dreadful deed was the more awful through the talented actress taking the fatal drug in the theatre itself. She had scarcely been taken home when to the universal grief, she expired. There is a rumour in the town that an unfortunate love affair drove her to this terrible act.'

Aratov slowly laid the paper on the table. In outward appearance he remained perfectly calm . . . but at once something seemed to strike him a blow in the chest and the head — and slowly the shock passed on through all his limbs. He got up, stood still on the spot, and sat down again, again read through the paragraph. Then he got up again, lay down on the bed, and clasping his hands behind, stared a long while at the wall, as though dazed. By degrees the wall seemed to fade away . . . vanished . . . and he saw facing him the boulevard under the grey sky, and *her* in her black cape . . . then her on the platform . . . saw himself even close by her. That something which had given him such a violent blow in the chest at the first instant, began mounting now . . . mounting into his throat. . . . He tried to clear his throat; tried to call some one—but his voice failed him—and, to his own astonishment, tears rushed in torrents from his eyes . . . what called forth these tears? Pity? Remorse? Or was it simply his nerves could not stand the sudden shock?

Why, she was nothing to him? was she?

'But, perhaps, it's not true after all,' the thought came as a sudden relief to him. 'I must find out! But from whom? From the princess? No, from Kupfer . . . from Kupfer? But they say he's not in Moscow—no matter, I must try him first!'

With these reflections in his head, Aratov dressed himself in haste, called a cab and drove to Kupfer's.

IX

THOUGH he had not expected to find him, he found him. Kupfer had, as a fact, been away from Moscow for some time, but he had now been back a week, and was indeed on the point of setting off to see Aratov. He met him with his usual heartiness, and was beginning to make some sort of explanation . . . but Aratov at once cut him short with the impatient question, 'Have you heard it? Is it true?'

'Is what true?' replied Kupfer, puzzled.

'About Clara Militch?'

Kupfer's face expressed commiseration. 'Yes, yes, my dear boy, it 's true; she poisoned herself! Such a sad thing!'

Aratov was silent for a while. 'But did you read it in the paper too?' he asked—'or perhaps you have been in Kazan yourself?'

'I have been in Kazan, yes; the princess and I accompanied her there. She came out on the stage there, and had a great success. But I didn't stay up to the time of the catastrophe . . . I was in Yaroslav at the time.'

'In Yaroslav?'

'Yes—I escorted the princess there. . . . She is living now at Yaroslav.'

'But you have trustworthy information?'

'Trustworthy . . . I have it at first-hand!—
I made the acquaintance of her family in
Kazan. But, my dear boy . . . this news seems
to be upsetting you? Why, I recollect you
didn't care for Clara at one time? You were
wrong, though! She was a marvellous girl—
only what a temper! I was terribly broken-
hearted about her!'

Aratov did not utter a word, he dropped into
a chair, and after a brief pause, asked Kupfer
to tell him . . . he stammered.

'What?' inquired Kupfer.

'Oh . . . everything,' Aratov answered
brokenly, 'all about her family . . . and the
rest of it. Everything you know!'

'Why, does it interest you? By all means!'
And Kupfer, whose face showed no traces of
his having been so terribly broken-hearted
about Clara, began his story.

From his account Aratov learnt that Clara
Militch's real name was Katerina Milovidov;
that her father, now dead, had held the post of
drawing-master in a school in Kazan, had
painted bad portraits and holy pictures of the
regulation type; that he had besides had the
character of being a drunkard and a domestic
tyrant; that he had left behind him, first a
widow, of a shopkeeper's family, a quite stupid

45

body, a character straight out of an Ostrovsky comedy; and secondly, a daughter much older than Clara and not like her—a very clever girl, and enthusiastic, only sickly, a remarkable girl —and very advanced in her ideas, my dear boy! That they were living, the widow and daughter, fairly comfortably, in a decent little house, obtained by the sale of the bad portraits and holy pictures; that Clara . . . or Katia, if you like, from her childhood up impressed every one with her talent, but was of an insubordinate, capricious temper, and used to be for ever quarrelling with her father; that having an inborn passion for the theatre, at sixteen she had run away from her parent's house with an actress . . .'

'With an actor?' put in Aratov.

'No, not with an actor, with an actress, to whom she became attached. . . . It's true this actress had a protector, a wealthy gentleman, no longer young, who did not marry her simply because he happened to be married—and indeed I fancy the actress was a married woman.' Furthermore Kupfer informed Aratov that Clara had even before her coming to Moscow acted and sung in provincial theatres, that, having lost her friend the actress—the gentleman, too, it seemed, had died, or else he had made it up with his wife—Kupfer could not quite remember this—she had made the acquaintance of the princess, 'that heart of gold, whom you, my dear Yakov Andreitch,' the speaker added with feeling, 'were incapable of appreciating properly'; that at last Clara had been offered an engagement in Kazan, and that she had accepted it, though before then she used to declare that she would never leave Moscow! But then how the people of Kazan liked her—it was really astonishing! Whatever the performance was, nothing but nosegays and presents! nosegays and presents! A wholesale miller, the greatest swell in the province, had even presented her with a gold inkstand! Kupfer related all this with great animation, without giving expression, however, to any special sentimentality, and interspersing his narrative with the questions, 'What is it to you?' and 'Why do you ask?' when Aratov, who listened to him with devouring attention, kept asking for more and more details. All was told at last, and Kupfer was silent, rewarding himself for his exertions with a cigar.

'And why did she take poison?' asked Aratov. 'In the paper it was stated . . .'

Kupfer waved his hand. 'Well . . . that I can't say . . . I don't know. But the paper tells a lie. Clara's conduct was exemplary

. . . no love affairs of any kind. . . . And indeed how should there be with her pride! She was proud—as Satan himself—and unapproachable! A headstrong creature! Hard as rock! You'll hardly believe it—though I knew her so well—I never saw a tear in her eyes!'

'But I have,' Aratov thought to himself.

'But there's one thing,' continued Kupfer, 'of late I noticed a great change in her: she grew so dull, so silent, for hours together there was no getting a word out of her. I asked her even, "Has any one offended you, Katerina Semyonovna?" For I knew her temper; she could never swallow an affront! But she was silent, and there was no doing anything with her! Even her triumphs on the stage didn't cheer her up; bouquets fairly showered on her . . . but she didn't even smile! She gave one look at the gold inkstand—and put it aside! She used to complain that no one had written the real part for her, as she conceived it. And her singing she'd given up altogether. It was my fault, my dear boy! . . . I told her that you thought she'd no musical knowledge, But for all that . . . why she poisoned herself—is incomprehensible! And the way she did it! . . .'

'In what part had she the greatest success?'

. . Aratov wanted to know in what part she had appeared for the last time, but for some reason he asked a different question.

'In Ostrovosky's *Gruna*, as far as I remember. But I tell you again she'd no love affairs! You may be sure of that from one thing. She lived in her mother's house. . . . You know the sort of shopkeeper's houses: in every corner a holy picture and a little lamp before it, a deadly stuffiness, a sour smell, nothing but chairs along the walls in the drawing-room, a geranium in the window, and if a visitor drops in, the mistress sighs and groans, as if they were invaded by an enemy. What chance is there for gallantry or love-making? Sometimes they wouldn't even admit me. Their servant, a muscular female, in a red sarafan, with an enormous bust, would stand right across the passage, and growl, "Where are you coming?" No, I positively can't understand why she poisoned herself. Sick of life, I suppose,' Kupfer concluded his cogitations philosophically.

Aratov sat with downcast head. 'Can you give me the address of that house in Kazan?' he said at last

'Yes; but what do you want it for? Do you want to write a letter there?'

'Perhaps.'

'Well, you know best But the old lady won't answer, for she can't read and write. The sister, though, perhaps . . . Oh, the sister's a clever creature! But I must say again, I wonder at you, my dear boy! Such indifference before . . . and now such interest! All this, my boy, comes from too much solitude!'

Aratov made no reply, and went away, having provided himself with the Kazan address.

When he was on his way to Kupfer's, excitement, bewilderment, expectation had been reflected on his face. . . . Now he walked with an even gait, with downcast eyes, and hat pulled over his brows; almost every one who met him sent a glance of curiosity after him . . . but he did not observe any one who passed . . . it was not as on the Tversky boulevard!

'Unhappy Clara! poor frantic Clara!' was echoing in his soul.

X

THE following day Aratov spent, however, fairly quietly. He was even able to give his mind to his ordinary occupations. But there was one thing: both during his work and during his leisure he was continually thinking of Clara, of what Kupfer had told him the evening before. It is true that his meditations, too, were of a fairly tranquil character. He fancied that this strange girl interested him from the psychological point of view, as something of the nature of a riddle, the solution of which was worth racking his brains over. 'Ran away with an actress living as a kept mistress,' he pondered, 'put herself under the protection of that princess, with whom she seems to have lived—and no *love affairs*? It's incredible! . . . Kupfer talked of pride! But in the first place we know' (Aratov ought to have said: we have read in books), . . . 'we know that pride can exist side by side with levity of conduct; and secondly, how came she, if she were so proud, to make an appointment with a man who might treat her with contempt . . . and did treat her with it . . . and in a public place, moreover . . . in a boulevard!' At this point Aratov recalled all the scene in the boulevard, and he asked himself, Had he really shown contempt for Clara?' 'No,' he decided, . . . 'it was another feeling . . . a feeling of doubt . . . lack of confidence, in fact!' 'Unhappy Clara!' was again ringing in his head. 'Yes, unhappy,' he decided again. . . . 'That's the most fitting word. And, if so, I was unjust. She said truly that I did not understand her.

A pity! Such a remarkable creature, perhaps, came so close. . . . and I did not take advantage of it, I repulsed her. . . . Well, no matter! Life's all before me. There will be, very likely, other meetings, perhaps more interesting!

'But on what grounds did she fix on *me* of all the world?' He glanced into a looking-glass by which he was passing. 'What is there special about me? I'm not a beauty, am I? My face . . . is like any face. . . . She was not a beauty either, though.

'Not a beauty . . . and such an expressive face! Immobile . . . and yet expressive! I never met such a face. . . . And talent, too, she has . . . that is, she had, unmistakable. Untrained, undeveloped, even coarse, perhaps . . . but unmistakable talent. And in that case I was unjust to her.' Aratov was carried back in thought to the literary musical matinée . . . and he observed to himself how exceedingly clearly he recollected every word she had sung or recited, every intonation of her voice. . . . 'That would not have been so had she been without talent. And now it is all in the grave, to which she has hastened of herself. . . . But I've nothing to do with that . . . I'm not to blame! It would be positively ridiculous to suppose that I'm to blame.'

It again occurred to Aratov that even if she

had had 'anything of the sort' in her mind, his behaviour during their interview must have effectually disillusioned her. . . . 'That was why she laughed so cruelly, too, at parting. Besides, what proof is there that she took poison because of unrequited love? That's only the newspaper correspondents, who ascribe every death of that sort to unrequited love! People of a character like Clara's readily feel life repulsive . . . burdensome. Yes, burdensome. Kupfer was right; she was simply sick of life.

'In spite of her successes, her triumphs?' Aratov mused. He got a positive pleasure from the psychological analysis to which he was devoting himself. Remote till now from all contact with women, he did not even suspect all the significance for himself of this intense realisation of a woman's soul.

'It follows,' he pursued his meditations, 'that art did not satisfy her, did not fill the void in her life. Real artists exist only for art, for the theatre. . . . Everything else is pale beside what they regard as their vocation. . . . She was a dilettante.'

At this point Aratov fell to pondering again. 'No, the word dilettante did not accord with that face, the expression of that face, those eyes. . . .'

And Clara's image floated again before him, with eyes, swimming in tears, fixed upon him, with clenched hands pressed to her lips. . . .

'Ah, no, no,' he muttered, 'what's the use?'

So passed the whole day. At dinner Aratov talked a great deal with Platosha, questioned her about the old days, which she remembered, but described very badly, as she had so few words at her command, and except her dear Yasha, had scarcely ever noticed anything in her life. She could only rejoice that he was nice and good-humoured to-day; towards evening Aratov was so far calm that he played several games of cards with his aunt.

So passed the day... but the night!

XI

IT began well; he soon fell asleep, and when his aunt went into him on tip-toe to make the sign of the cross three times over him in his sleep—she did so every night—he lay breathing as quietly as a child. But before dawn he had a dream.

He dreamed he was on a bare steppe, strewn with big stones, under a lowering sky. Among the stones curved a little path; he walked along it.

Suddenly there rose up in front of him something of the nature of a thin cloud. He looked steadily at it; the cloud turned into a woman in a white gown with a bright sash round her waist She was hurrying away from him. He saw neither her face nor her hair . . . they were covered by a long veil. But he had an intense desire to overtake her, and to look into her face. Only, however much he hastened, she went more quickly than he.

On the path lay a broad flat stone, like a tombstone. It blocked up the way. The woman stopped. Aratov ran up to her; but yet he could not see her eyes . . . they were shut. Her face was white, white as snow; her hands hung lifeless. She was like a statue.

Slowly, without bending a single limb, she fell backwards, and sank down upon the tombstone. . . . And then Aratov lay down beside her, stretched out straight like a figure on a monument, his hands folded like a dead man's.

But now the woman suddenly rose, and went away. Aratov tried to get up too . . . but he could neither stir nor unclasp his hands, and could only gaze after her in despair.

Then the woman suddenly turned round, and he saw bright living eyes, in a living but unknown face. She laughed, she waved her hand to him . . . and still he could not move.

She laughed once more, and quickly retreated, merrily nodding her head, on which there was a crimson wreath of tiny roses.

Aratov tried to cry out, tried to throw off this awful nightmare. . . .

Suddenly all was darkness around . . . and the woman came back to him. But this was not the unknown statue . . . it was Clara. She stood before him, crossed her arms, and sternly and intently looked at him. Her lips were tightly pressed together, but Aratov fancied he heard the words, 'If you want to know what I am, come over here!'

'Where?' he asked.

'Here!' he heard the wailing answer. 'Here!'

Aratov woke up.

He sat up in bed, lighted the candle that stood on the little table by his bedside—but did not get up—and sat a long while, chill all over, slowly looking about him. It seemed to him as if something had happened to him since he went to bed; that something had taken possession of him . . . something was in control of him. 'But is it possible?' he murmured unconsciously. 'Does such a power really exist?'

He could not stay in his bed. He quickly

dressed, and till morning he was pacing up and down his room. And, strange to say, of Clara he never thought for a moment, and did not think of her, because he had decided to go next day to Kazan!

He thought only of the journey, of how to manage it, and what to take with him, and how he would investigate and find out everything there, and would set his mind at rest. 'If I don't go,' he reasoned with himself, 'why, I shall go out of my mind!' He was afraid of that, afraid of his nerves. He was convinced that when once he had seen everything there with his own eyes, every obsession would vanish like that nightmare. 'And it will be a week lost over the journey,' he thought; 'what is a week? else I shall never shake it off.'

The rising sun shone into his room; but the light of day did not drive away the shadows of the night that lay upon him, and did not change his resolution.

Platosha almost had a fit when he informed her of his intention. She positively sat down on the ground . . . her legs gave way beneath her. 'To Kazan? why to Kazan?' she murmured, her dim eyes round with astonishment She would not have been more surprised if she had been told that her Yasha was going to marry the baker woman next door, or was starting for America. 'Will you be long in Kazan?' 'I shall be back in a week,' answered Aratov, standing with his back half-turned to his aunt, who was still sitting on the floor.

Platonida Ivanova tried to protest more, but Aratov answered her in an utterly unexpected and unheard-of way: 'I'm not a child,' he shouted, and he turned pale all over, his lips trembled, and his eyes glittered wrathfully. 'I'm twenty-six, I know what I'm about, I'm free to do what I like! I suffer no one . . . Give me the money for the journey, pack my box with my clothes and linen . . . and don't torture me! I'll be back in a week, Platosha,' he added, in a somewhat softer tone.

Platosha got up, sighing and groaning, and, without further protest, crawled to her room. Yasha had alarmed her. 'I've no head on my shoulders,' she told the cook, who was helping her to pack Yasha's things; 'no head at all, but a hive full of bees all a-buz and a-hum! He's going off to Kazan, my good soul, to Ka-a-zan!' The cook, who had observed their dvornik the previous evening talking for a long time with a police officer, would have liked to inform her mistress of this circumstance, but did not dare, and only reflected, 'To Kazan! if only it's nowhere farther still!' Platonida

Ivanovna was so upset that she did not even utter her usual prayer. 'In such a calamity the Lord God Himself cannot aid us!'

The same day Aratov set off for Kazan.

XII

HE had no sooner reached that town and taken a room in a hotel than he rushed off to find out the house of the widow Milovidov. During the whole journey he had been in a sort of benumbed condition, which had not, however, prevented him from taking all the necessary steps, changing at Nizhni-Novgorod from the railway to the steamer, getting his meals at the stations etc., etc. He was convinced as before that *there* everything would be solved; and therefore he drove away every sort of memory and reflection, confining himself to one thing, the mental rehearsal of the *speech*, in which he would lay before the family of Clara Militch the real cause of his visit. And now at last he reached the goal of his efforts, and sent up his name. He was admitted . . . with perplexity and alarm—still he was admitted.

The house of the widow Milovidov turned out to be exactly as Kupfer had described it;

and the widow herself really was like one of the tradesmen's wives in Ostrovsky, though the widow of an official; her husband had held his post under government. Not without some difficulty, Aratov, after a preliminary apology for his boldness, for the strangeness of his visit, delivered the speech he had prepared, explaining that he was anxious to collect all the information possible about the gifted artist so early lost, that he was not led to this by idle curiosity, but by profound sympathy for her talent, of which he was the devoted admirer (he said that, devoted admirer!) that, in fact, it would be a sin to leave the public in ignorance of what it had lost—and why its hopes were not realised. Madame Milovidov did not interrupt Aratov; she did not understand very well what this unknown visitor was saying to her, and merely opened her eyes rather wide and rolled them upon him, thinking, however, that he had a quiet respectable air, was well dressed . . . and not a pickpocket . . . hadn't come to beg.

'You are speaking of Katia?' she inquired, directly Aratov was silent

'Yes . . . of your daughter.'

'And you have come from Moscow for this?'

'Yes, from Moscow.'

'Only on this account?'

'Yes.'

Madame Milovidov gave herself a sudden shake. 'Why, are you an author? Do you write for the newspapers?'

'No, I'm not an author—and hitherto I have not written for the newspapers.'

The widow bowed her head. She was puzzled.

'Then, I suppose . . . it's from your own interest in the matter?' she asked suddenly. Aratov could not find an answer for a minute.

'Through sympathy, from respect for talent,' he said at last.

The word 'respect' pleased Madame Milovidov. 'Eh!' she pronounced with a sigh . . . 'I'm her mother, any way—and terribly I'm grieved for her. . . . Such a calamity all of a sudden! . . . But I must say it: a crazy girl she always was—and what a way to meet with her end! Such a disgrace. . . . Only fancy what it was for a mother? we must be thankful indeed that they gave her a Christian burial. . . .' Madame Milovidov crossed herself. 'From a child up she minded no one—she left her parent's house . . . and at last—sad to say!— turned actress! Every one knows I never shut my doors upon her; I loved her, to be sure! I was her mother, any way! she 'd no need to live with strangers . . . or to go begging! . . .' Here the widow shed tears . . . 'But if you, my good sir,' she began, again wiping her eyes with the ends of her kerchief, 'really have any idea of the kind, and you are not intending anything dishonourable to us, but on the contrary, wish to show us respect, you'd better talk a bit with my other daughter. Shell tell you everything better than I can. . . . Annotchka! called Madame Milovidov, 'Annotchka, come here! Here is a worthy gentleman from Moscow wants to have a talk about Katia!'

There was a sound of something moving in the next room; but no one appeared. 'Annotchka!' the widow called again, 'Anna Semyonovna! come here, I tell you!'

The door softly opened, and in the doorway appeared a girl no longer very young, looking ill—and plain—but with very soft and mournful eyes. Aratov got up from his seat to meet her, and introduced himself, mentioning his friend Kupfer. 'Ah! Fyodor Fedoritch?' the girl articulated softly, and softly she sank into a chair.

'Now, then, you must talk to the gentleman,' said Madam Milovidov, getting up heavily: 'he 's taken trouble enough, he 's come all the way from Moscow on purpose—he wants to collect information about Katia. And will you, my good sir,' she added, addressing Aratov —'excuse me . . . I'm going to look after my housekeeping. You can get a very good

62

account of everything from Annotchka; she will tell you about the theatre. . . . and all the rest of it. She is a clever girl, well educated: speaks French, and reads books, as well as her sister did. One may say indeed she gave her her education . . . she was older—and so she looked after it.'

Madame Milovidov withdrew. On being left alone with Anna Semyonovna, Aratov repeated his speech to her; but realising at the first glance that he had to do with a really cultivated girl, not a typical tradesman's daughter, he went a little more into particulars and made use of different expressions; but towards the end he grew agitated, flushed and felt that his heart was throbbing. Anna listened to him in silence, her hands folded on her lap; a mournful smile never left her face . . . bitter grief, still fresh in its poignancy, was expressed in that smile.

'You knew my sister?' she asked Aratov.

'No, I did not actually know her,' he answered. 'I met her and heard her once . . . but one need only hear and see your sister once to . . .'

'Do you wish to write her biography?' Anna questioned him again.

Aratov had not expected this inquiry; however, he replied promptly, 'Why not? But above all, I wanted to acquaint the public . . .'

Anna stopped him by a motion of her hand.
'What is the object of that? The public
caused her plenty of suffering as it is; and indeed Katia had only just begun life. But if
you yourself—(Anna looked at him and smiled
again a smile as mournful but more friendly
. . . as though she were saying to herself, Yes,
you make me feel I can trust you) . . . if you
yourself feel such interest in her, let me ask you
to come and see us this afternoon . . . after
dinner. I can't just now . . . so suddenly . . .
I will collect my strength . . . I will make an
effort . . . Ah, I loved her too much!'

Anna turned away; she was on the point of
bursting into sobs.

Aratov rose hurriedly from his seat, thanked
her for her offer, said he should be sure . . . oh,
very sure!—to come—and went off, carrying
away with him an impression of a soft voice,
gentle and sorrowful eyes, and burning in the
tortures of expectation.

XIII

ARATOV went back the same day to the Milovidovs and spent three whole hours in conversation with Anna Semyonovna. Madame Milovi-

dov was in the habit of lying down directly after dinner—at two o'clock—and resting till evening tea at seven. Aratov's talk with Clara's sister was not exactly a conversation; she did almost all the talking, at first with hesitation, with embarrassment, then with a warmth that refused to be stifled. It was obvious that she had adored her sister. The confidence Aratov had inspired in her grew and strengthened; she was no longer stiff; twice she even dropped a few silent tears before him. He seemed to her to be worthy to hear an unreserved account of all she knew and felt . . . in her own secluded life nothing of this sort had ever happened before! . . . As for him . . . he drank in every word she uttered.

This was what he learned . . . much of it of course, half-said . . . much he filled in for himself.

In her early years, Clara had undoubtedly been a disagreeable child; and even as a girl, she had not been much gentler; self-willed, hot-tempered, sensitive, she had never got on with her father, whom she despised for his drunkenness and incapacity. He felt this and never forgave her for it. A gift for music showed itself early in her; her father gave it no encouragement, acknowledging no art but painting, in which he himself was so conspicuously

65

unsuccessful though it was the means of support of himself and his family. Her mother Clara loved, . . . but in a careless way, as though she were her nurse; her sister she adored, though she fought with her and had even bitten her. . . . It is true she fell on her knees afterwards and kissed the place she had bitten. She was all fire, all passion, and all contradiction; revengeful and kind; magnanimous and vindictive; she believed in fate—and did not believe in God (these words Anna whispered with horror); she loved everything beautiful, but never troubled herself about her own looks, and dressed anyhow; she could not bear to have young men courting her, and yet in books she only read the pages which treated of love; she did not care to be liked, did not like caresses, but never forgot a caress, just as she never forgot a slight; she was afraid of death and killed herself! She used to say sometimes, 'Such a one as I want I shall never meet . . . and no other will I have!' 'Well, but if you meet him?' Anna would ask. 'If I meet him . . . I will capture him.' 'And if he won't let himself be captured?' 'Well, then . . . I will make an end of myself. It will prove I am no good.' Clara's father—he used sometimes when drunk to ask his wife, 'Who got you your blackbrowed she-devil there? Not I!'—Clara's

66

father, anxious to get her off his hands as soon
as possible, betrothed her to a rich young shopkeeper, a great blockhead, one of the so-called
'refined' sort A fortnight before the wedding-
day—she was only sixteen at the time—she
went up to her betrothed, her arms folded and
her fingers drumming on her elbows—her
favourite position—and suddenly gave him a
slap on his rosy cheek with her large powerful
hand! He jumped and merely gaped; it must
be said he was head over ears in love with her
. . . He asked: 'What's that for?' She
laughed scornfully and walked off. 'I was
there in the room,' Anna related, 'I saw it all,
I ran after her and said to her, "Katia, why did
you do that, really?" And she answered me:
"If he'd been a real man he would have punished me, but he's no more pluck than a
drowned hen! And then he asks, 'What 's that
for?' If he loves me, and doesn't bear malice.
he had better put up with it and not ask,
'What's that for?' I will never be anything to
him—never, never! "And indeed she did not
marry him. It was soon after that she made
the acquaintance of that actress, and left her
home. Mother cried, but father only said, "A
stubborn beast is best away from the flock!"
And he did not bother about her, or try to find
her out My father did not understand Katia.

67

On the day before her flight, 'added Anna,' she almost smothered me in her embraces, and kept repeating: "I can't, I can't help it! . . . My heart's torn, but I can't help it! your cage is too small . . . it cramps my wings! And there's no escaping one's fate. . . ."

'After that,' observed Anna, 'we saw each other very seldom. . . . When my father died, she came for a couple of days, would take nothing of her inheritance, and vanished again. She was unhappy with us . . . I could see that Afterwards she came to Kazan as an actress.'

Aratov began questioning Anna about the theatre, about the parts in which Clara had appeared, about her triumphs. . . . Anna answered in detail, but with the same mournful, though keen fervour. She even showed Aratov a photograph, in which Clara had been taken, in the costume of one of her parts. In the photograph she was looking away, as though tnrning from the spectators; her thick hair tied with a ribbon fell in a coil on her bare arm. Aratov looked a long time at the photograph, thought it like, asked whether Clara had taken part in public recitations, and learnt that she had not; that she had needed the excitement of the theatre, the scenery . . . but another question was burning on his lips.

'Anna Semyonovna!' he cried at last, not

loudly, but with a peculiar force, 'tell me, I implore you, tell me why did she . . . what led her to this fearful step?' . . .

Anna looked down. 'I don't know,' she said, after a pause of some instants. 'By God, I don't know!' she went on strenuously, supposing from Aratov's gesture that he did not believe her. . . . 'since she came back here certainly she was melancholy, depressed. Something must have happened to her in Moscow—what, I could never guess. But on the other hand, on that fatal day she seemed as it were . . . if not more cheerful, at least more serene than usual. Even I had no presentiment,' added Anna with a bitter smile, as though reproaching herself for it.

'You see,' she began again, 'it seemed as though at Katia's birth it had been decreed that she was to be unhappy. From her early years she was convinced of it. She would lean her head on her hand, sink into thought, and say, "I shall not live long!" She used to have presentiments. Imagine! she used to see beforehand, sometimes in a dream and sometimes awake, what was going to happen to her! "If I can't live as I want to live, then I won't live," . . . was a saying of hers too. . . . "Our life's in our own hands, you know." And she proved that!'

Anna hid her face in her hands and stopped speaking. 'Anna Semyonovna,' Aratov began after a short pause, 'you have perhaps heard to what the newspapers ascribed . . . "To an unhappy love affair?"' Anna broke in, at once pulling away her hands from her face. 'That's a slander, a fabrication! . . . My pure, un-approachable Katia . . . Katia! . . . and unhappy, unrequited love? And shouldn't I have known of it? . . . Every one was in love with her . . . while she . . . And whom could she have fallen in love with here? Who among all the people here, who was worthy of her? Who was up to the standard of honesty, truth, purity . . . yes, above all, of purity which she, with all her faults, always held up as an ideal before her? . . . She repulsed! . . . she! . . .'

Anna's voice broke. . . . Her fingers were trembling. All at once she flushed crimson . . . crimson with indignation, and for that instant, and that instant only, she was like her sister.

Aratov was beginning an apology.

'Listen,' Anna broke in again. 'I have an intense desire that you should not believe that slander, and should refute it, if possible! You want to write an article or something about her: that's your opportunity for defending her memory! That's why I talk so openly to you. Let me tell you; Katia left a diary . . .'

Aratov trembled. 'A diary?' he muttered.
'Yes, a diary . . . that is, only a few pages.
Katia was not fond of writing . . . for months
at a time she would write nothing, and her
letters were so short But she was always,
always truthful, she never told a lie. . . . She,
with her pride, tell a lie! I . . . I will show
you this diary! You shall see for yourself
whether there is the least hint in it of any unhappy love affair!'

Anna quickly took out of a table-drawer a
thin exercise-book, ten pages, no more, and
held it out to Aratov. He seized it eagerly,
recognised the irregular sprawling handwriting,
the handwriting of that anonymous letter,
opened it at random, and at once lighted upon
the following lines.

'Moscow, Tuesday . . . June—Sang and
recited at a literary matinée. To-day is a vital
day for me. *It must decide my fate.* (These
words were twice underlined.) I saw again . . .'
Here followed a few lines carefully erased.
And then, 'No! no! no! . . . Must go back
to the old way, if only . . .'

Aratov dropped the hand that held the diary,
and his head slowly sank upon his breast

'Read it!' cried Anna. 'Why don't you
read it? Read it through from the beginning.
. . . It would take only five minutes to read it

all, though the diary extends over two years. In Kazan she used to write down nothing at all. . . .'

Aratov got up slowly from his chair and flung himself on his knees before Anna.

She was simply petrified with wonder and dismay.

'Give me . . . give me that diary,' Aratov began with failing voice, and he stretched out both hands to Anna. 'Give it me . . . and the photograph . . . you are sure to have some other one, and the diary I will return. . . . But I want it, oh, I want it! . . .'

In his imploring words, in his contorted features there was something so despairing that it looked positively like rage, like agony . . . And he was in agony, truly. He could not himself have foreseen that such pain could be felt by him, and in a frenzy he implored forgiveness, deliverance . . .

'Give it me,' he repeated.

'But . . . you . . . you were in love with my sister?' Anna said at last.

Aratov was still on his knees.

'I only saw her twice . . . believe me! . . . and if I had not been impelled by causes, which I can neither explain nor fully understand myself, . . . if there had not been some power over me, stronger than myself. . . . I should not be entreating you . . . I should not have come here. I want . . . I must . . . you yourself said I ought to defend her memory!'

'And you were not in love with my sister?' Anna asked a second time.

Aratov did not at once reply, and he turned aside a little, as though in pain.

'Well, then! I was! I was—I'm in love now,' he cried in the same tone of despair.

Steps were heard in the next room.

'Get up . . . get up . . .' said Anna hurriedly. 'Mamma is coming.'

Aratov rose.

'And take the diary and the photograph, in God's name! Poor, poor Katia! . . . But you will give me back the diary,' she added emphatically. 'And if you write anything, be sure to send it me. . . . Do you hear?'

The entrance of Madame Milovidov saved Aratov from the necessity of a reply. He had time, however, to murmur, 'You are an angel! Thanks! I will send anything I write. . . .'

Madame Milovidov, half awake, did not suspect anything. So Aratov left Kazan with the photograph in the breast-pocket of his coat The diary he gave back to Anna; but, unobserved by her, he cut out the page on which were the words underlined.

On the way back to Moscow he relapsed

again into a state of petrifaction. Though he was secretly delighted that he had attained the object of his journey, still all thoughts of Clara he deferred till he should be back at home. He thought much more about her sister Anna. 'There,' he thought, 'is an exquisite, charming creature. What delicate comprehension of everything, what a loving heart, what a complete absence of egoism! And how girls like that spring up among us, in the provinces, and in such surroundings too! She is not strong, and not good-looking, and not young; but what a splendid helpmate she would be for a sensible, cultivated man! That's the girl I ought to have fallen in love with!' Such were Aratov's reflections... but on his arrival in Moscow things put on quite a different complexion.

XIV

PLATONIDA IVANOVNA was unspeakably rejoiced at her nephew's return. There was no terrible chance she had not imagined during his absence. 'Siberia at least!' she muttered, sitting rigidly still in her little room; 'at least for a year!' The cook too had terrified her by the most well-authenticated stories of the disappearance of this and that young man of the neighbourhood. The perfect innocence and absence of revolutionary ideas in Yasha did not in the least reassure the old lady. 'For indeed . . . if you come to that, he studies photography . . . and that's quite enough for them to arrest him!' And behold, here was her darling Yasha back again, safe and sound. She observed, indeed, that he seemed thinner, and looked hollow in the face; natural enough, with no one to look after him! but she did not venture to question him about his journey. She asked at dinner. 'And is Kazan a fine town?' 'Yes,' answered Aratov. 'I suppose they're all Tartars living there?' 'Not only Tartars.' 'And did you get a Kazan dressing-gown while you were there?' 'No, I didn't.' With that the conversation ended.

But as soon as Aratov found himself alone in his own room, he quickly felt as though something were enfolding him about, as though he were once more *in the power*, yes, in the power of another life, another being. Though he had indeed said to Anna in that sudden delirious outburst that he was in love with Clara, that saying struck even him now as senseless and frantic. No, he was not in love; and how could he be in love with a dead woman, whom he had not even liked in her lifetime, whom he had almost for-

75

gotten? No, but he was in *her* power . . .
he no longer belonged to himself. He was
captured. So completely captured, that he did
not even attempt to free himself by laughing at
his own absurdity, nor by trying to arouse if
not a conviction, at least a hope in himself that
it would all pass, that it was nothing but nerves,
nor by seeking for proofs, nor by anything!
'If I meet him, I will capture him,' he recalled
those words of Clara's Anna had repeated to him.
Well, he was captured. But was not she dead?
Yes, her body was dead . . . but her soul?. . . .
is not that immortal? . . . does it need corporeal
organs to show its power? Magnetism has
proved to us the influence of one living human
soul over another living human soul. . . . Why
should not this influence last after death, if the
soul remains living? But to what end? What
can come of it? But can we, as a rule, appre-
hend what is the object of all that takes place
about us? These ideas so absorbed Aratov that
he suddenly asked Platosha at tea-time whether
she believed in the immortality of the soul. She
did not for the first minute understand what
his question was, then she crossed herself and
answered. 'She should think so indeed! The
soul not immortal!' 'And, if so, can it have
any influence after death?' Aratov asked again.
The old lady replied that it could . . . pray

for us, that is to say; at least, when it had passed through all its ordeals, awaiting the last dread judgment. But for the first forty days the soul simply hovered about the place where its death had occurred.

'The first forty days?'

'Yes; and then the ordeals follow.'

Aratov was astounded at his aunt's knowledge, and went off to his room. And again he felt the same thing, the same power over him. This power showed itself in Clara's image being constantly before him to the minutest details, such details as he seemed hardly to have observed in her lifetime; he saw . . . saw her fingers, her nails, the little hairs on her cheeks near her temples, the little mole under her left eye; he saw the slight movement of her lips, her nostrils, her eyebrows . . . and her walk, and how she held her head a little on the right side . . . he saw everything. He did not by any means take a delight in it all, only he could not help thinking of it and seeing it. The first night after his return he did not, however, dream of her . . . he was very tired, and slept like a log. But directly he waked up, she came back into his room again, and seemed to establish herself in it, as though she were the mistress, as though by her voluntary death she had purchased the right to it, without asking him or needing his

77

permission. He took up her photograph, he began reproducing it, enlarging it Then he took it into his head to fit it to the stereoscope. He had a great deal of trouble to do it . . . at last he succeeded. He fairly shuddered when through the glass he looked upon her figure, with the semblance of corporeal solidity given it by the stereoscope. But the figure was grey, as though covered with dust . . . and moreover the eyes—the eyes looked always to one side, as though turning away. A long, long while he stared at them, as though expecting them to turn to him . . . he even half-closed his eyelids on purpose . . . but the eyes remained immovable, and the whole figure had the look of some sort of doll. He moved away, flung himself in an armchair, took out the leaf from her diary, with the words underlined, and thought, 'Well, lovers, they say, kiss the words traced by the hand of the beloved—but I feel no inclination to do that—and the handwriting I think ugly. But that line contains my sentence.' Then he recalled the promise he had made Anna about the article. He sat down to the table, and set to work upon it, but everything he wrote struck him as so false, so rhetorical . . . especially so false . . . as though he did not believe in what he was writing nor in his own feelings. . . . And Clara herself seemed so utterly unknown and uncomprehended! She seemed to withhold herself from him. 'No!' he thought, throwing down the pen . . . 'either authorship's altogether not my line, or I must wait a little!' He fell to recalling his visit to the Milovidovs, and all Anna had told him, that sweet, delightful Anna. . . . A word she had uttered—'pure'—suddenly struck him. It was as though something scorched him, and shed light. 'Yes,' he said aloud, 'she was pure, and I am pure. . . . That's what gave her this power.'

Thoughts of the immortality of the soul, of the life beyond the grave crowded upon him again. Was it not said in the Bible: 'Death, where is thy sting?' And in Schiller: 'And the dead shall live!' (Auch die Todten sollen leben!)

And too, he thought, in Mitskevitch: 'I will love thee to the end of time . . . and beyond it!' And an English writer had said: 'Love is stronger than death.' The text from Scripture produced particular effect on Aratov. . . . He tried to find the place where the words occurred. . . . He had no Bible; he went to ask Platosha for one. She wondered, she brought out, however, a very old book in a warped leather binding, with copper clasps, covered with candle wax, and handed it over to

Aratov. He bore it off to his own room, but for a long time he could not find the text . . . he stumbled, however, on another: 'Greater love hath no man than this, that a man lay down his life for his friends' (S. John xv. 13).

He thought: 'That's not right. It ought to be: Greater *power* hath no man.'

'But if she did not lay down her life for me at all? If she made an end of herself simply because life had become a burden to her? What if, after all, she did not come to that meeting for anything to do with love at all?'

But at that instant he pictured to himself Clara before their parting on the boulevard. . . . He remembered the look of pain on her face, and the tears and the words, 'Ah, you understood nothing!'

No! he could have no doubt why and for whom she had laid down her life. . . .

So passed that whole day till night-time.

XV

ARATOV went to bed early, without feeling specially sleepy, but he hoped to find repose in bed. The strained condition of his nerves brought about an exhaustion far more unbearable than the bodily fatigue of the journey and the railway. However, exhausted as he was, he could not get to sleep. He tried to read . . . but the lines danced before his eyes. He put out the candle, and darkness reigned in his room. But still he lay sleepless, with his eyes shut. . . . And it began to seem to him some one was whispering in his ear. . . . 'The beating of the heart, the pulse of the blood,' he thought. . . . But the whisper passed into connected speech. Some one was talking in Russian hurriedly, plaintively, and indistinctly. Not one separate word could he catch. . . . But it was the voice of Clara.

Aratov opened his eyes, raised himself, leaned on his elbow. . . . The voice grew fainter, but kept up its plaintive, hurried talk, indistinct as before. . . .

It was unmistakably Clara's voice.

Unseen fingers ran light arpeggios up and down the keys of the piano . . . then the voice began again. More prolonged sounds were audible . . . as it were moans . . . always the same over and over again. Then apart from the rest the words began to stand out . . . 'Roses . . . roses . . . roses. . . .'

'Roses,' repeated Aratov in a whisper. 'Ah, yes! it's the roses I saw on that woman's head in the dream.' . . . 'Roses,' he heard again.

'Is that you?' Aratov asked in the same whisper. The voice suddenly ceased.

Aratov waited . . . and waited, and dropped his head on the pillow. 'Hallucinations of hearing,' he thought. 'But if . . . if she really were here, close at hand? . . . If I were to see her, should I be frightened? or glad? But what should I be frightened of? or glad of? Why, of this, to be sure; it would be a proof that there is another world, that the soul is immortal. Though, indeed, even if I did see something, it too might be a hallucination of the sight. . . .'

He lighted the candle, however, and in a rapid glance, not without a certain dread, scanned the whole room . . . and saw nothing in it unusual. He got up, went to the stereoscope . . . again the same grey doll, with its eyes averted. The feeling of dread gave way to one of annoyance. He was, as it were, cheated in his expectations . . . the very expectation indeed struck him as absurd.

'Well, this is positively idiotic!' he muttered, as he got back into bed, and blew out the candle. Profound darkness reigned once more.

Aratov resolved to go to sleep this time. . . . But a fresh sensation started up in him. He fancied some one was standing in the middle of the room, not far from him, and scarcely perceptibly breathing. He turned round hastily and opened his eyes. . . . But what could be seen in impenetrable darkness? He began to feel for a match on his little bedside table . . . and suddenly it seemed to him that a sort of soft, noiseless hurricane was passing over the whole room, over him, through him, and the word 'I!' sounded distinctly in his ears. . . .

'I! . . . I!' . . .

Some instants passed before he succeeded in getting the candle alight.

Again there was no one in the room; and he now heard nothing, except the uneven throbbing of his own heart. He drank a glass of water, and stayed still, his head resting on his hand. He was waiting.

He thought: 'I will wait. Either it's all nonsense . . . or she is here. She is not going to play cat and mouse with me like this!' He waited, waited long . . . so long that the hand on which he was resting his head went numb . . . but not one of his previous sensations was repeated. Twice his eyes closed. . . . He opened them promptly . . . at least he believed that he opened them. Gradually they turned towards the door and rested on it The candle burned dim, and it was once more dark in the room . . . but the door made a long streak of white in the half darkness. And now this patch began to move, to grow less, to disappear . . . and in its place, in the doorway appeared a woman's figure. Aratov looked intently at it . . . Clara! And this time she was looking straight at him, coming towards him. . . . On her head was a wreath of red roses. . . . He was all in agitation, he sat up. . . .

Before him stood his aunt in a nightcap adorned with a broad red ribbon, and in a white dressing-jacket.

'Platosha!' he said with an effort. 'Is that you?'

'Yes, it's I,' answered Platonida Ivanovna . . . 'I, Yasha darling, yes.'

'What have you come for?'

'You waked me up. At first you kept moaning as it were . . . and then you cried out all of a sudden, "Save me! help me!"'

'I cried out?'

'Yes, and such a hoarse cry, "Save me!" I thought, Mercy on us! He's never ill, is he? And I came in. Are you quite well?'

'Perfectly well.'

'Well, you must have had a bad dream then. Would you like me to burn a little incense?'

Aratov once more stared intently at his aunt, and laughed aloud. . . . The figure of the good old lady in her nightcap and dressing-jacket, with her long face and scared expression, was

certainly very comic. All the mystery surrounding him, oppressing him—everything
weird was sent flying instantaneously.

'No, Platosha dear, there 's no need,' he said.
'Please forgive me for unwittingly troubling
you. Sleep well, and I will sleep too.'

Platonida Ivanovna remained a minute
standing where she was, pointed to the candle,
grumbled, 'Why not put it out . . . an accident
happens in a minute?' and as she went out,
could not refrain, though only at a distance,
from making the sign of the cross over him.

Aratov fell asleep quickly, and slept till
morning. He even got up in a happy frame
of mind . . . though he felt sorry for something. . . . He felt light and free. 'What
romantic fancies, if you come to think of it!'
he said to himself with a smile. He never
once glanced either at the stereoscope, or at
the page torn out of the diary. Immediately
after breakfast, however, he set off to go to
Kupfer's.

What drew him there . . . he was dimly
aware.

XVI

ARATOV found his sanguine friend at home.
He chatted a little with him, reproached him

for having quite forgotten his aunt and himself, listened to fresh praises of that heart of gold, the princess, who had just sent Kupfer from Yaroslav a smoking-cap embroidered with fish-scales . . . and all at once, sitting just opposite Kupfer and looking him straight in the face, he announced that he had been a journey to Kazan.

'You have been to Kazan; what for?'

'Oh, I wanted to collect some facts about that . . . Clara Militch.'

'The one that poisoned herself?'

'Yes.'

Kupfer shook his head. 'Well, you are a chap! And so quiet about it! Toiled a thousand miles out there and back . . . for what? Eh?? If there 'd been some woman in the case now! Then I can understand anything! anything! any madness!' Kupfer ruffled up his hair. 'But simply to collect materials, as it's called among you learned people. . . . I 'd rather be excused! There are statistical writers to do that job! Well, and did you make friends with the old lady and the sister? Isn't she a delightful girl?'

'Delightful,' answered Aratov, 'she gave me a great deal of interesting information.'

'Did she tell you exactly how Clara took poison?

'You mean . . . how?'

'Yes, in what manner?'

'No . . . she was still in such grief . . . I did not venture to question her too much. Was there anything remarkable about it?'

'To be sure there was. Only fancy; she had to appear on the stage that very day, and she acted her part. She took a glass of poison to the theatre with her, drank it before the first act, and went through all that act afterwards. With the poison inside her! Isn't that something like strength of will? Character, eh?? And, they say, she never acted her part with such feeling, such passion! The public suspected nothing, they clapped, and called for her. . . . And directly the curtain fell, she dropped down there, on the stage. Convulsions . . . and convulsions, and within an hour she was dead! But didn't I tell you all about it? And it was in the papers too!'

Aratov's hands had grown suddenly cold, and he felt an inward shiver.

'No, you didn't tell me that,' he said at last 'And you don't know what play it was?

Kupfer thought a minute. 'I did hear what the play was . . . there is a betrayed girl in it . . . Some drama, it must have been. Clara was created for dramatic parts. . . . Her very appearance . . . But where are you off

to?' Kupfer interrupted himself, seeing that
Aratov was reaching after his hat.

'I don't feel quite well,' replied Aratov.
'Good-bye . . . I'll come in another time.'

Kupfer stopped him and looked into his face.
'What a nervous fellow you are, my boy! Just
look at yourself. . . . You're as white as
chalk.

'I'm not well,' repeated Aratov, and, dis-
engaging himself from Kupfer's detaining
hands, he started homewards. Only at that
instant it became clear to him that he had
come to Kupfer with the sole object of talking
of Clara . . .

'Unhappy Clara, poor frantic Clara. . . .'

On reaching home, however, he quickly
regained his composure to a certain degree.

The circumstances accompanying Clara's
death had at first given him a violent shock
. . . but later on this performance 'with the
poison inside her,' as Kupfer had expressed it,
struck him as a kind of monstrous pose, a piece
of bravado, and he was already trying not to
think about it, fearing to arouse a feeling in himself, not unlike repugnance. And at dinner, as
he sat facing Platosha, he suddenly recalled her
midnight appearance, recalled that abbreviated
dressing-jacket, the cap with the high ribbon—

and why a ribbon on a nightcap?—all the ludicrous apparition which, like the scene-shifter's whistle in a transformation scene, had dissolved all his visions into dust! He even forced Platosha to repeat her description of how she had heard his scream, had been alarmed, had jumped up, could not for a minute find either his door or her own, and so on. In the evening he played a game of cards with her, and went off to his room rather depressed, but again fairly composed.

Aratov did not think about the approaching night, and was not afraid of it: he was sure he would pass an excellent night The thought of Clara had sprung up within him from time to time; but he remembered at once how 'affectedly' she had killed herself, and turned away from it. This piece of 'bad taste' blocked out all other memories of her. Glancing cursorily into the stereoscope, he even fancied that she was averting her eyes because she was ashamed. Opposite the stereoscope on the wall hung a portrait of his mother. Aratov took it from its nail, scrutinised it a long while, kissed it and carefully put it away in a drawer. Why did he do that? Whether it was that it was not fitting for this portrait to be so close to that woman . . . or for some other reason Aratov did not inquire of himself.

But his mother's portrait stirred up memories of his father . . . of his father, whom he had seen dying in this very room, in this bed. 'What do you think of all this, father?' he mentally addressed himself to him. 'You understand all this; you too believed in Schiller's world of spirits. Give me advice!'

'Father would have advised me to give up all this idiocy,' Aratov said aloud, and he took up a book. He could not, however, read for long, and feeling a sort of heaviness all over, he went to bed earlier than usual, in the full conviction that he would fall asleep at once.

And so it happened . . . but his hopes of a quiet night were not realised.

XVII

IT had not struck midnight when he had an extraordinary and terrifying dream.

He dreamed that he was in a rich manor-house of which he was the owner. He had lately bought both the house and the estate attached to it. And he kept thinking, 'It's nice, very nice now, but evil is coming!' Beside him moved to and fro a little tiny man, his steward; he kept laughing, bowing, and

trying to show Aratov how admirably everything was arranged in his house and his estate.
'This way, pray, this way, pray,' he kept repeating, chuckling at every word; 'kindly look
how prosperous everything is with you! Look
at the horses . . . what splendid horses!' And
Aratov saw a row of immense horses. They
were standing in their stalls with their backs to
him; their manes and tails were magnificent
. . . but as soon as Aratov went near, the
horses' heads turned towards him, and they
showed their teeth viciously. 'It's very nice,'
Aratov thought! 'but evil is coming!' 'This
way, pray, this way,' the steward repeated
again, 'pray come into the garden: look what
fine apples you have! 'The apples certainly
were fine, red, and round; but as soon as
Aratov looked at them, thcy withered and fell
. . . 'Evil is coming,' he thought. 'And here is
the lake,' lisped the steward, 'isn't it blue and
smooth? And here's a little boat of gold . . .
will you get into it? . . . it floats of itself.'
'I won't get into it,' thought Aratov, 'evil is
coming!' and for all that he got into the boat.
At the bottom lay huddled up a little creature
like a monkey; it was holding in its paws a
glass full of a dark liquid. 'Pray don't be
uneasy,' the steward shouted from the bank . . .
'It's of no consequence! It's death! Good

luck to you! 'The boat darted swiftly along
. . . but all of a sudden a hurricane came
swooping down on it, not like the hurricane
of the night before, soft and noiseless—no; a
black, awful, howling hurricane! Everything
was confusion. And in the midst of the
whirling darkness Aratov saw Clara in a
stage-dress; she was lifting a glass to her lips,
listening to shouts of 'Bravo! bravo!' in the
distance, and some coarse voice shouted in
Aratov's ear: 'Ah! did you think it would
all end in a farce? No; it's a tragedy! a
tragedy!'

Trembling all over, Aratov awoke. In the
room it was not dark. . . . A faint light
streamed in from somewhere, and showed every
thing in the gloom and stillness. Aratov did
not ask himself whence this light came. . . .
He felt one thing only: Clara was there, in
that room . . . he felt her presence . . . he
was again and for ever in her power!

The cry broke from his lips, 'Clara, are you
here?'

'Yes!' sounded distinctly in the midst of the
lighted, still room.

Aratov inaudibly repeated his question. . . .

'Yes!' he heard again.

'Then I want to see you!' he cried, and he
jumped out of bed.

For some instants he stood in the same place, pressing his bare feet on the chill floor. His eyes strayed about. 'Where? where?' his lips were murmuring. . . .

Nothing to be seen, not a sound to be heard. . . . He looked round him, and noticed that the faint light that filled the room came from a night-light, shaded by a sheet of paper and set in a corner, probably by Platosha while he was asleep. He even discerned the smell of incense . . . also, most likely, the work of her hands.

He hurriedly dressed himself: to remain in bed, to sleep, was not to be thought of. Then he took his stand in the middle of the room, and folded his arms. The sense of Clara's presence was stronger in him than it had ever been.

And now he began to speak, not loudly, but with solemn deliberation, as though he were uttering an incantation.

'Clara,' he began, 'if you are truly here, if you see me, if you hear me—show yourself! . . . If the power which I feel over me is truly your power, show yourself! If you understand how bitterly I repent that I did not understand you, that I repelled you—show yourself! If what I have heard was truly your voice; if the feeling overmastering me is love; if you are now convinced that I love you, I, who till now have

93

neither loved nor known any woman; if you know that since your death I have come to love you passionately, inconsolably; if you do not want me to go mad,—show yourself, Clara!'

Aratov had hardly uttered this last word, when all at once he felt that some one was swiftly approaching him from behind—as that day on the boulevard—and laying a hand on his shoulder. He turned round, and saw no one. But the sense of *her* presence had grown so distinct, so unmistakable, that once more he looked hurriedly about him. . . .

What was that? On an easy-chair, two paces from him, sat a woman, all in black. Her head was turned away, as in the stereoscope. . . . It was she! It was Clara! But what a stern, sad face!

Aratov slowly sank on his knees. Yes; he was right, then. He felt neither fear nor delight, not even astonishment. . . . His heart even began to beat more quietly. He had one sense, one feeling, 'Ah! at last! at last!'

'Clara,' he began, in a faint but steady voice, 'why do you not look at me? I know that it is you . . . but I may fancy my imagination has created an image like *that one* . . .'—he pointed towards the stereoscope—'prove to me that it is you. . . . Turn to me, look at me, Clara!'

Clara's hand slowly rose . . . and fell again.
'Clara! Clara! turn to me!'

And Clara's head slowly turned, her closed
lids opened, and her dark eyes fastened upon
Aratov.

He fell back a little, and uttered a single,
long-drawn-out, trembling 'Ah!'

Clara gazed fixedly at him . . . but her eyes,
her features, retained their former mournfully
stern, almost displeased expression. With just
that expression on her face she had come on to
the platform on the day of the literary matinée,
before she caught sight of Aratov. And, just
as then, she suddenly flushed, her face bright-
ened, her eyes kindled, and a joyful, triumphant
smile parted her lips. . . .

'I have come!' cried Aratov. 'You have
conquered. . . . Take me! I am yours, and
you are mine!'

He flew to her; he tried to kiss those smiling,
triumphant lips, and he kissed them. He felt
their burning touch: he even felt the moist
chill of her teeth: and a cry of triumph rang
through the half-dark room.

Platonida Ivanovna, running in, found him in
a swoon. He was on his knees; his head was
lying on the arm-chair; his outstretched arms
hung powerless; his pale face was radiant with
the intoxication of boundless bliss.

Platonida Ivanovna fairly dropped to the ground beside him; she put her arms round him, faltered, 'Yasha! Yasha, darling! Yasha, dearest!' tried to lift him in her bony arms . . . he did not stir. Then Platonida Ivanovna fell to screaming in a voice unlike her own. The servant ran in. Together they somehow roused him, began throwing water over him—even took it from the holy lamp before the holy picture. . . .

He came to himself. But in response to his aunt's questions he only smiled, and with such an ecstatic face that she was more alarmed than ever, and kept crossing first herself and then him. . . . Aratov, at last, put aside her hand, and, still with the same ecstatic expression of face, said: 'Why, Platosha, what is the matter with you?'

'What is the matter with you, Yasha darling?'

'With me? I am happy . . . happy, Platosha . . . That's what 's the matter with me. And now I want to lie down, to sleep. . . .' He tried to get up, but felt such a sense of weakness in his legs, and in his whole body, that he could not, without the help of his aunt and the servant, undress and get into bed. But he fell asleep very quickly, still with the same look of blissful triumph on his face. Only his face was very pale.

XVIII

WHEN Platonida Ivanovna came in to him next morning, he was still in the same position . . . but the weakness had not passed off and he actually preferred to remain in bed. Platonida Ivanovna did not like the pallor of his face at all. 'Lord, have mercy on us! what is it?' she thought; 'not a drop of blood in his face, refuses broth, lies there and smiles, and keeps declaring he's perfectly well!' He refused breakfast too. 'What is the matter with you, Yasha?' she questioned him; 'do you mean to lie in bed all day?' 'And what if I did?' Aratov answered gently. This very gentleness again Platonida Ivanovna did not like at all. Aratov had the air of a man who has discovered a great, very delightful secret, and is jealously guarding it and keeping it to himself. He was looking forward to the night, not impatiently, but with curiosity. 'What next?' he was asking himself; 'what will happen?' Astonishment, incredulity, he had ceased to feel; he did not doubt that he was in communication with Clara, that they loved one another . . . that, too, he had no doubt about. Only . . . what could come of such love? He recalled that kiss . . . and a delicious shiver ran swiftly and sweetly through all his limbs. 'Such a kiss,' was his thought, 'even Romeo and Juliet knew not! But next time I will be stronger. . . . I will master her. . . . She shall come with a wreath of tiny roses in her dark curls. . . .

'But what next? We cannot live together, can we? Then must I die so as to be with her? Is it not for that she has come; and is it not *so* she means to take me captive?

'Well; what then? If I must die, let me die. Death has no terrors for me now. It cannot, then, annihilate me? On the contrary, only *thus* and *there* can I be happy . . . as I have not been happy in life, as she has not. . . . We are both pure! Oh, that kiss!'

Platonida Ivanovna was incessantly coming into Aratov's room. She did not worry him with questions; she merely looked at him, muttered, sighed, and went out again. But he refused his dinner too: this was really too dreadful. The old lady set off to an acquaintance of hers, a district doctor, in whom she placed some confidence, simply because he did not drink and had a German wife. Aratov was surprised when she brought him in to see him; but Platonida Ivanovna so earnestly implored

her darling Yashenka to allow Paramon Paramonitch (that was the doctor's name) to
examine him—if only for her sake—that
Aratov consented. Paramon Paramonitch felt
his pulse, looked at his tongue, asked a question, and announced at last that it was absolutely
necessary for him to 'auscultate' him. Aratov
was in such an amiable frame of mind that he
agreed to this too. The doctor delicately
uncovered his chest, delicately tapped, listened,
hummed and hawed, prescribed some drops
and a mixture, and, above all, advised him to
keep quiet and avoid any excitement. 'I dare
say!' thought Aratov; 'that idea's a little too
late, my good friend!' 'What is wrong with
Yasha?' queried Platonida Ivanovna, as she
slipped a three-rouble note into Paramon
Paramonitch's hand in the doorway. The
district doctor, who like all modern physicians
—especially those who wear a government uniform—was fond of showing off with scientific
terms, announced that her nephew's diagnosis
showed all the symptoms of neurotic cardialgia,
and there were febrile symptoms also. 'Speak
plainer, my dear sir; do,' cut in Platonida
Ivanovna; 'don't terrify me with your Latin;
you're not in your surgery!' 'His heart's not
right, the doctor explained; 'and, well—there's
a little fever too' . . . and he repeated his

99

advice as to perfect quiet and absence of excitement. 'But there's no danger, is there?' Platonida Ivanovna inquired severely ('You dare rush off into Latin again,' she implied.) 'No need to anticipate any at present!'

The doctor went away . . . and Platonida Ivanovna grieved. . . . She sent to the surgery, though, for the medicine, which Aratov would not take, in spite of her entreaties. He refused any herb-tea too. 'And why are you so uneasy, dear?' he said to her; 'I assure you, I'm at this moment the sanest and happiest man in the whole world!' Platonida Ivanovna could only shake her head. Towards evening he grew rather feverish; and still he insisted that she should not stay in his room, but should go to sleep in her own. Platonida Ivanovna obeyed; but she did not undress, and did not lie down. She sat in an arm-chair, and was all the while listening and murmuring her prayers.

She was just beginning to doze, when suddenly she was awakened by a terrible piercing shriek. She jumped up, rushed into Aratov's room, and as on the night before, found him lying on the floor.

But he did not come to himself as on the previous night, in spite of all they could do. He fell the same night into a high fever, complicated by failure of the heart

A few days later he passed away.

A strange circumstance attended his second fainting-fit. When they lifted him up and laid him on his bed, in his clenched right hand they found a small tress of a woman's dark hair. Where did this lock of hair come from? Anna Semyonovna had such a lock of hair left by Clara; but what could induce her to give Aratov a relic so precious to her? Could she have put it somewhere in the diary, and not have noticed it when she lent the book?

In the delirium that preceded his death, Aratov spoke of himself as Romeo . . . after the poison; spoke of marriage, completed and perfect; of his knowing now what rapture meant Most terrible of all for Platosha was the minute when Aratov, coming a little to himself, and seeing her beside his bed, said to her, 'Aunt, what are you crying for?—because I must die? But don't you know that love is stronger than death? . . . Death! death! where is thy sting? You should not weep, but rejoice, even as I rejoice. . . .'

And once more on the face of the dying man shone out the rapturous smile, which gave the poor old woman such cruel pain.

PHANTOMS

*'One instant . . . and the fairy tale is over,
And once again the actual fills the soul. . . .'* —A. FET.

PHANTOMS

I

For a long time I could not get to sleep, and kept turning from side to side. Confound this foolishness about table-turning! 'I thought. 'It simply upsets one's nerves.' . . . Drowsiness began to overtake me at last. . . .

Suddenly it seemed to me as though there were the faint and plaintive sound of a harp-string in the room.

I raised my head. The moon was low in the sky, and looked me straight in the face. White as chalk lay its light upon the floor. . . . The strange sound was distinctly repeated.

I leaned on my elbow. A faint feeling of awe plucked at my heart. A minute passed, another. . . . Somewhere, far away, a cock crowed; another answered still more remote.

I let my head sink back on the pillow. 'See what one can work oneself up to,' I thought again, . . . 'there's a singing in my ears.'

After a little while I fell asleep—or I thought

I fell asleep. I had an extraordinary dream. I fancied I was lying in my room, in my bed—and was not asleep, could not even close my eyes. And again I heard the sound. . . . I turned over. . . . The moonlight on the floor began softly to lift, to rise up, to round off slightly above. . . . Before me, impalpable as mist, a white woman was standing motionless.

'Who are you?' I asked with an effort.

A voice made answer, like the rustle of leaves: 'It is I . . . I . . . I . . . I have come for you.'

'For me? But who are you?'

'Come by night to the edge of the wood where there stands an old oak-tree. I will be there.'

I tried to look closely into the face of the mysterious woman—and suddenly I gave an involuntary shudder: there was a chilly breath upon me. And then I was not lying down, but sitting up in my bed; and where, as I fancied, the phantom had stood, the moonlight lay in a long streak of white upon the floor.

II

THE day passed somehow. I tried, I remember, to read, to work . . . everything was a failure. The night came. My heart was throbbing

within me, as though it expected something.
I lay down, and turned with my face to the
wall.

'Why did you not come?' sounded a distinct
whisper in the room.

I looked round quickly.

Again she . . . again the mysterious phantom.
Motionless eyes in a motionless face, and a
gaze full of sadness.

'Come!' I heard the whisper again.

'I will come,' I replied with instinctive
horror. The phantom bent slowly forward,
and undulating faintly like smoke, melted away
altogether. And again the moon shone white
and untroubled on the smooth floor.

III

I PASSED the day in unrest. At supper I drank
almost a whole bottle of wine, and all but went
out on to the steps; but I turned back and
flung myself into my bed. My blood was
pulsing painfully.

Again the sound was heard . . . I started,
but did not look round. All at once I felt that
some one had tight hold of me from behind, and
was whispering in my very ear: 'Come, come,

come.' . . . Trembling with terror, I moaned out: 'I will come!' and sat up.

A woman stood stooping close to my very pillow. She smiled dimly and vanished. I had time, though, to make out her face. It seemed to me I had seen her before—but where, when? I got up late, and spent the whole day wandering about the country. I went to the old oak at the edge of the forest, and looked carefully all around.

Towards evening I sat at the open window in my study. My old housekeeper set a cup of tea before me, but I did not touch it. . . . I kept asking myself in bewilderment: 'Am not I going out of my mind?' The sun had just set: and not the sky alone was flushed with red; the whole atmosphere was suddenly filled with an almost unnatural purple. The leaves and grass never stirred, stiff as though freshly coated with varnish. In their stony rigidity, in the vivid sharpness of their outlines, in this combination of intense brightness and death-like stillness, there was something weird and mysterious. A rather large grey bird suddenly flew up without a sound and settled on the very window sill. . . . I looked at it, and it looked at me sideways with its round, dark eye. 'Were you sent to remind me, then?' I wondered.

At once the bird fluttered its soft wings, and without a sound—as before—flew away. I sat a long time still at the window, but I was no longer a prey to uncertainty. I had, as it were, come within the enchanted circle, and I was borne along by an irresistible though gentle force, as a boat is borne along by the current long before it reaches the waterfall. I started up at last. The purple had long vanished from the air, the colours were darkened, and the enchanted silence was broken. There was the flutter of a gust of wind, the moon came out brighter and brighter in the sky that was growing bluer, and soon the leaves of the trees were weaving patterns of black and silver in her cold beams. My old housekeeper came into the study with a lighted candle, but there was a draught from the window and the flame went out. I could restrain myself no longer. I jumped up, clapped on my cap, and set off to the corner of the forest, to the old oak-tree.

IV

THIS oak had, many years before, been struck by lightning; the top of the tree had been shattered, and was withered up, but there was still life left in it for centuries to come. As I was coming up to it, a cloud passed over the moon: it was very dark under its thick branches. At first I noticed nothing special; but I glanced on one side, and my heart fairly failed me—a white figure was standing motionless beside a tall bush between the oak and the forest My hair stood upright on my head, but I plucked up my courage and went towards the forest.

Yes, it was she, my visitor of the night. As I approached her, the moon shone out again. She seemed all, as it were, spun out of half-transparent, milky mist,—through her face I could see a branch faintly stirring in the wind; only the hair and eyes were a little dark, and on one of the fingers of her clasped hands a slender ring shone with a gleam of pale gold. I stood still before her, and tried to speak; but the voice died away in my throat, though it was no longer fear exactly I felt. Her eyes were turned upon me; their gaze expressed neither distress nor delight, but a sort of lifeless attention. I waited to see whether she would utter a word, but she remained motionless and speechless, and still gazed at me with her deathly intent eyes. Dread came over me again.

'I have come!' I cried at last with an effort. My voice sounded muffled and strange to me.

'I love you,' I heard her whisper.

'You love me!' I repeated in amazement.

'Give yourself up to me,' was whispered me again in reply.

'Give myself up to you! But you are a phantom; you have no body even.' A strange animation came upon me. 'What are you—smoke, air, vapour? Give myself up to you! Answer me first, Who are you? Have you lived upon the earth? Whence have you come?'

'Give yourself up to me. I will do you no harm. Only say two words: "Take me."'

I looked at her. 'What is she saying?' I thought. 'What does it all mean? And how can she take me? Shall I try?'

'Very well,' I said, and unexpectedly loudly, as though some one had given me a push from behind; 'take me!'

I had hardly uttered these words when the mysterious figure, with a sort of inward laugh, which set her face quivering for an instant, bent forward, and stretched out her arms wide apart. . . . I tried to dart away, but I was already in her power. She seized me, my body rose a foot from the ground, and we both floated smoothly and not too swiftly over the wet, still grass.

V

AT first I felt giddy, and instinctively I closed
my eyes. . . . A minute later I opened them
again. We were floating as before; but the
forest was now nowhere to be seen. Under us
stretched a plain, spotted here and there with
dark patches. With horror I felt that we had
risen to a fearful height.

'I am lost; I am in the power of Satan,'
flashed through me like lightning. Till that
instant the idea of a temptation of the evil one,
of the possibility of perdition, had never entered
my head. We still whirled on, and seemed to
be mounting higher and higher.

'Where will you take me?' I moaned at last.

'Where you like,' my companion answered

She clung close to me; her face was almost
resting upon my face. But I was scarcely conscious of her touch.

'Let me sink down to the earth, I am giddy
at this height.'

'Very well; only shut your eyes and hold
your breath.'

I obeyed, and at once felt that I was falling
like a stone flung from the hand . . . the air
whistled in my ears. When I could think

again, we were floating smoothly once more just above the earth, so that we caught our feet in the tops of the tall grass.

'Put me on my feet,' I began. 'What pleasure is there in flying? I'm not a bird.'

'I thought you would like it. We have no other pastime.'

'You? Then what are you?'

There was no answer.

'You don't dare to tell me that?'

The plaintive sound which had awakened me the first night quivered in my ears. Meanwhile we were still, scarcely perceptibly, moving in the damp night air.

'Let me go!' I said. My companion moved slowly away, and I found myself on my feet She stopped before me and again folded her hands. I grew more composed and looked into her face; as before it expressed submissive sadness.

'Where are we?' I asked. I did not recognise the country about me.

'Far from your home, but you can be there in an instant.'

'How can that be done? by trusting myself to you again?'

'I have done you no harm and will do you none. Let us fly till dawn, that is all. I can bear you away wherever you fancy—to the ends of the earth. Give yourself up to me! Say only: "Take me!"'

'Well . . . take me!'

She again pressed close to me, again my feet left the earth— and we were flying.

VI

'Which way?' she asked me.

'Straight on, keep straight on.'

'But here is a forest.'

'Lift us over the forest, only slower.'

We darted upwards like a wild snipe flying up into a birch-tree, and again flew on in a straight line. Instead of grass, we caught glimpses of tree-tops just under our feet. It was strange to see the forest from above, its bristling back lighted up by the moon. It looked like some huge slumbering wild beast, and accompanied us with a vast unceasing murmur, like some inarticulate roar. In one place we crossed a small glade; intensely black was the jagged streak of shadow along one side of it Now and then there was the plaintive cry of a hare below us; above us the owl hooted, plaintively too; there was a scent in the air of mushrooms, buds, and

dawn-flowers; the moon fairly flooded everything on all sides with its cold, hard light; the
Pleiades gleamed just over our heads. And
now the forest was left behind; a streak of
fog stretched out across the open country; it
was the river. We flew along one of its banks,
above the bushes, still and weighed down with
moisture. The river's waters at one moment
glimmered with a flash of blue, at another
flowed on in darkness, as it were, in wrath.
Here and there a delicate mist moved strangely
over the water, and the water-lilies' cups shone
white in maiden pomp with every petal open
to its full, as though they knew their safety out
of reach. I longed to pick one of them, and
behold, I found myself at once on the river's
surface . . . The damp air struck me an angry
blow in the face, just as I broke the thick stalk
of a great flower. We began to fly across from
bank to bank, like the water-fowl we were
continually waking up and chasing before us.
More than once we chanced to swoop down on
a family of wild ducks, settled in a circle on an
open spot among the reeds, but they did not
stir; at most one of them would thrust out
its neck from under its wing, stare at us, and
anxiously poke its beak away again in its
fluffy feathers, and another faintly quacked, while
its body twitched a little all over. We startled

one heron; it flew up out of a willow bush, brandishing its legs and fluttering its wings with clumsy eagerness: it struck me as remarkably like a German. There was not the splash of a fish to be heard, they too were asleep. I began to get used to the sensation of flying, and even to find a pleasure in it; any one will understand me, who has experienced flying in dreams. I proceeded to scrutinise with close attention the strange being, by whose good offices such unlikely adventures had befallen me.

VII

SHE was a woman with a small un-Russian face. Greyish-white, half-transparent, with scarcely marked shades, she reminded one of the alabaster figures on a vase lighted up within, and again her face seemed familiar to me.

'Can I speak with you?' I asked.

'Speak.'

'I see a ring on your finger; you have lived then on the earth, you have been married?'

I waited . . . There was no answer.

'What is your name, or, at least, what was it?'

'Call me Alice.'

'Alice! That's an English name! Are you an Englishwoman? Did you know me in former days?'

'No.'

'Why is it then you have come to me?'

'I love you.'

'And are you content?'

'Yes; we float, we whirl together in the fresh air.'

'Alice!' I said all at once, 'you are perhaps a sinful, condemned soul?'

My companion's head bent towards me. 'I don't understand you,' she murmured.

'I adjure you in God's name . . .' I was beginning.

'What are you saying?' she put in in perplexity. 'I don't understand.'

I fancied that the arm that lay like a chilly girdle about my waist softly trembled . . .

'Don't be afraid,' said Alice, 'don't be afraid, my dear one!' Her face turned and moved towards my face. . . . I felt on my lips a strange sensation, like the faintest prick of a soft and delicate sting. . . . Leeches might prick so in mild and drowsy mood.

VIII

I GLANCED downwards. We had now risen again to a considerable height. We were flying over some provincial town I did not know, situated on the side of a wide slope. Churches rose up high among the dark mass of wooden roofs and orchards; a long bridge stood out black at the bend of a river; everything was hushed, buried in slumber. The very crosses and cupolas seemed to gleam with a silent brilliance; silently stood the tall posts of the wells beside the round tops of the willows; silently the straight whitish road darted arrow-like into one end of the town, and silently it ran out again at the opposite end on to the dark waste of monotonous fields.

'What town is this?' I asked.

'X ...'

'X ... in Y ... province?'

'Yes.'

'I'm a long distance indeed from home!'

'Distance is not for us.'

'Really?' I was fired by a sudden recklessness. 'Then take me to South America!

'To America I cannot It's daylight there by now.'

'And we are night-birds. Well, anywhere, where you can, only far, far away.'

'Shut your eyes and hold your breath,' answered Alice, and we flew along with the speed of a whirlwind. With a deafening noise the air rushed into my ears. We stopped, but the noise did not cease. On the contrary, it changed into a sort of menacing roar, the roll of thunder . . .

'Now you can open your eyes,' said Alice.

IX

I OBEYED . . . Good God, where was I?

Overhead, ponderous, smoke-like storm-clouds; they huddled, they moved on like a herd of furious monsters . . . and there below, another monster; a raging, yes, raging, sea . . . The white foam gleamed with spasmodic fury, and surged up in hillocks upon it, and hurling up shaggy billows, it beat with a sullen roar against a huge cliff, black as pitch. The howling of the tempest, the chilling gasp of the storm-rocked abyss, the weighty splash of the breakers, in which from time to time one fancied something like a wail, like distant cannon-shots, like a bell ringing—the tearing crunch and grind of the shingle on the beach, the sudden shriek of an unseen gull, on the murky horizon the disabled hulk of a ship—on every side death, death and horror . . . Giddiness overcame me, and I shut my eyes again with a sinking heart . . .

'What is this? Where are we?'

'On the south coast of the Isle of Wight opposite the Blackgang cliff where ships are so often wrecked,' said Alice, speaking this time with peculiar distinctness, and as it seemed to me with a certain malignant pleasure . . .

'Take me away, away from here . . . home! home!' I shrank up, hid my face in my hands . . . I felt that we were moving faster than before; the wind now was not roaring or moaning, it whistled in my hair, in my clothes . . . I caught my breath . . .

'Stand on your feet now,' I heard Alice's voice saying. I tried to master myself, to regain consciousness . . . I felt the earth under the soles of my feet, and I heard nothing, as though everything had swooned away about me . . . only in my temples the blood throbbed irregularly, and my head was still giddy with a faint ringing in my ears. I drew myself up and opened my eyes.

X

WE were on the bank of my pond. Straight before me there were glimpses through the pointed leaves of the willows of its broad surface with threads of fluffy mist clinging here and there upon it. To the right a field of rye shone dimly; on the left stood up my orchard trees, tall, rigid, drenched it seemed in dew . . . The breath of the morning was already upon them. Across the pure grey sky stretched like streaks of smoke, two or three slanting clouds; they had a yellowish tinge, the first faint glow of dawn fell on them; one could not say whence it came; the eye could not detect on the horizon, which was gradually growing lighter, the spot where the sun was to rise. The stars had disappeared; nothing was astir yet, though everything was already on the point of awakening in the enchanted stillness of the morning twilight.

'Morning! see, it is morning!' cried Alice in my ear. 'Farewell till to-morrow.'

I turned round . . . Lightly rising from the earth, she floated by, and suddenly she raised both hands above her head. The head and hands and shoulders glowed for an instant with warm, corporeal light; living sparks gleamed in the dark eyes; a smile of mysterious tenderness stirred the reddening lips. . . . A lovely woman had suddenly arisen before me. . . . But as though dropping into a swoon, she fell back instantly and melted away like vapour.

I remained passive.

When I recovered myself and looked round me, it seemed to me that the corporeal, pale-rosy colour that had flitted over the figure of my phantom had not yet vanished, and was enfolding me, diffused in the air. . . . It was the flush of dawn. All at once I was conscious of extreme fatigue and turned homewards. As I passed the poultry-yard, I heard the first morning cackling of the geese (no birds wake earlier than they do); along the roof at the end of each beam sat a rook, and they were all busily and silently pluming themselves, standing out in sharp outline against the milky sky. From time to time they all rose at once, and after a short flight, settled again in a row, without uttering a caw. . . . From the wood close by came twice repeated the drowsy, fresh chuck-chuck of the black-cock, beginning to fly into the dewy grass, overgrown by brambles. . . . With a faint tremor all over me I made my way to my bed, and soon fell into a sound sleep.

XI

THE next night, as I was approaching the old oak, Alice moved to meet me, as if I were an old friend. I was not afraid of her as I had been the day before, I was almost rejoiced at seeing her; I did not even attempt to comprehend what was happening to me; I was simply longing to fly farther to interesting places.

Alice's arm again twined about me, and we took flight again.

'Let us go to Italy,' I whispered in her ear.

'Wherever you wish, my dear one,' she answered solemnly and slowly, and slowly and solemnly she turned her face towards me. It struck me as less transparent than on the eve; more womanlike and more imposing; it recalled to me the being I had had a glimpse of in the early dawn at parting.

'This night is a great night,' Alice went on. 'It comes rarely—when seven times thirteen . . .'

At this point I could not catch a few words.

'To-night we can see what is hidden at other times.'

'Alice!' I implored, 'but who are you, tell me at last?'

Silently she lifted her long white hand. In the dark sky, where her finger was pointing, a comet flashed, a reddish streak among the tiny stars.

'How am I to understand you?' I began, 'Or, as that comet floats between the planets and the sun, do you float among men . . . or what?'

But Alice's hand was suddenly passed before my eyes . . . It was as though a white mist from the damp valley had fallen on me. . .

'To Italy! to Italy!' I heard her whisper. 'This night is a great night!'

XII

THE mist cleared away from before my eyes, and I saw below me an immense plain. But already, by the mere breath of the warm soft air upon my cheeks, I could tell I was not in Russia; and the plain, too, was not like our Russian plains. It was a vast dark expanse, apparently desert and not overgrown with grass; here and there over its whole extent gleamed pools of water, like broken pieces of looking-glass; in the distance could be dimly descried a noiseless motionless sea. Great stars shone bright in the spaces between the big beautiful clouds; the murmur of thousands, subdued but never-ceasing, rose on all sides, and very strange was this shrill but drowsy chorus, this voice of the darkness and the desert . . .

'The Pontine marshes,' said Alice. 'Do you hear the frogs? do you smell the sulphur?'

'The Pontine marshes . . .' I repeated, and a sense of grandeur and of desolation came upon me. 'But why have you brought me here, to this gloomy forsaken place? Let us fly to Rome instead.'

'Rome is near,' answered Alice. . . . 'Prepare yourself!'

We sank lower, and flew along an ancient Roman road. A bullock slowly lifted from the slimy mud its shaggy monstrous head, with short tufts of bristles between its crooked backward-bent horns. It turned the whites of its dull malignant eyes askance, and sniffed a heavy snorting breath into its wet nostrils, as though scenting us.

'Rome, Rome is near . . .' whispered Alice. 'Look, look in front. . . .'

I raised my eyes.

What was the blur of black on the edge of the night sky? Were these the lofty arches of an immense bridge? What river did it span?

Why was it broken down in parts? No, it was
not a bridge, it was an ancient aqueduct. All
around was the holy ground of the Campagna,
and there, in the distance, the Albanian hills,
and their peaks and the grey ridge of the old
aqueduct gleamed dimly in the beams of the
rising moon. . . .

We suddenly darted upwards, and floated in
the air before a deserted ruin. No one could
have said what it had been: sepulchre, palace,
or castle. . . . Dark ivy encircled it all over in
its deadly clasp, and below gaped yawning a
half-ruined vault. A heavy underground smell
rose in my face from this heap of tiny closely-
fitted stones, whence the granite facing of the
wall had long crumbled away.

'Here,' Alice pronounced, and she raised her
hand: 'Here! call aloud three times running
the name of the mighty Roman!'

'What will happen?'

'You will see.'

I wondered. *'Divus Caius Julius Caesar!*
I cried suddenly;' *'divus Caius Julius Caesar!*
I repeated deliberately; *'Caesar!'*

XIII

THE last echoes of my voice had hardly died away, when I heard . . .

It is difficult to say what I did hear. At first there reached me a confused din the ear could scarcely catch, the endlessly-repeated clamour of the blare of trumpets, and the clapping of hands. It seemed that somewhere, immensely far away, at some fathomless depth, a multitude innumerable was suddenly astir, and was rising up, rising up in agitation, calling to one another, faintly, as if muffled in sleep, the suffocating sleep of ages. Then the air began moving in dark currents over the ruin . . . . Shades began flitting before me, myriads of shades, millions of outlines, the rounded curves of helmets, the long straight lines of lances; the moonbeams were broken into momentary gleams of blue upon these helmets and lances, and all this army, this multitude, came closer and closer, and grew, in more and more rapid movement. . . . An indescribable force, a force fit to set the whole world moving, could be felt in it; but not one figure stood out clearly. . . . And suddenly I fancied a sort of tremor ran all round, as if it were the rush and rolling apart of some huge waves. . . .

'*Caesar, Caesar venit!*' sounded voices, like the leaves of a forest when a storm has suddenly broken upon it . . . a muffled shout thundered through the multitude, and a pale stern head, in a wreath of laurel, with downcast eyelids, the head of the emperor, began slowly to rise out of the ruin. . . .

There is no word in the tongue of man to express the horror which clutched at my heart. . . . I felt that were that head to raise its eyes, to part its lips, I must perish on the spot! 'Alice!' I moaned, 'I won't, I can't, I don't want Rome, coarse, terrible Rome. . . . Away, away from here!'

'Coward!' she whispered, and away we flew. I just had time to hear behind me the iron voice of the legions, like a peal of thunder . . . then all was darkness.

XIV

'Look round,' Alice said to me, 'and don't fear.'

I obeyed—and, I remember, my first impression was so sweet that I could only sigh. A sort of smoky-grey, silvery-soft, half-light, half-mist, enveloped me on all sides. At first

I made out nothing: I was dazzled by this
azure brilliance; but little by little began to
emerge the outlines of beautiful mountains and
forests; a lake lay at my feet, with stars
quivering in its depths, and the musical plash
of waves. The fragrance of orange flowers
met me with a rush, and with it—and also as
it were with a rush—came floating the pure
powerful notes of a woman's young voice.
This fragrance, this music, fairly drew me
downwards, and I began to sink . . . to sink
down towards a magnificent marble palace,
which stood, invitingly white, in the midst of
a wood of cypress. The music flowed out
from its wide open windows, the waves of the
lake, flecked with the pollen of flowers, splashed
upon its walls, and just opposite, all clothed in
the dark green of orange flowers and laurels,
enveloped in shining mist, and studded with
statues, slender columns, and the porticoes of
temples, a lofty round island rose out of the
water. . . .

'I sola Bella!' said Alice. . . . 'Lago
Maggiore. . . .'

I murmured only 'Ah!' and continued to
drop. The woman's voice sounded louder and
clearer in the palace; I was irresistibly drawn
towards it. . . . I wanted to look at the face of
the singer, who, in such music, gave voice to

such a night. We stood still before the window.

In the centre of a room, furnished in the style of Pompeii, and more like an ancient temple than a modern drawing-room, surrounded by Greek statues, Etruscan vases, rare plants, and precious stuffs, lighted up by the soft radiance of two lamps enclosed in crystal globes, a young woman was sitting at the piano. Her head slightly bowed and her eyes half-closed, she sang an Italian melody; she sang and smiled, and at the same time her face wore an expression of gravity, almost of sternness . . . a token of perfect rapture! She smiled . . . and Praxiteles' Faun, indolent, youthful as she, effeminate, and voluptuous, seemed to smile back at her from a corner, under the branches of an oleander, across the delicate smoke that curled upwards from a bronze censer on an antique tripod. The beautiful singer was alone. Spell-bound by the music, her beauty, the splendour and sweet fragrance of the night, moved to the heart by the picture of this youthful, serene, and untroubled happiness, I utterly forgot my companion, I forgot the strange way in which I had become a witness of this life, so remote, so completely apart from me, and I was on the point of tapping at the window, of speaking. . . .

I was set trembling all over by a violent shock—just as though I had touched a galvanic battery. I looked round. . . . The face of Alice was—for all its transparency—dark and menacing; there was a dull glow of anger in her eyes, which were suddenly wide and round. . . .

'Away!' she murmured wrathfully, and again whirling and darkness and giddiness. . . . Only this time not the shout of legions, but the voice of the singer, breaking on a high note, lingered in my ears. . . .

We stopped. The high note, the same note was still ringing and did not cease to ring in my ears, though I was breathing quite a different air, a different scent . . . a breeze was blowing upon me, fresh and invigorating, as though from a great river, and there was a smell of hay, smoke and hemp. The long-drawn-out note was followed by a second, and a third, but with an expression so unmistakable, a trill so familiar, so peculiarly our own, that I said to myself at once: 'That's a Russian singing a Russian song!' and at that very instant everything grew clear about me.

XV

WE found ourselves on a flat riverside plain. To the left, newly-mown meadows, with rows of huge hayricks, stretched endlessly till they were lost in the distance; to the right extended the smooth surface of a vast mighty river, till it too was lost in the distance. Not far from the bank, big dark barges slowly rocked at anchor, slightly tilting their slender masts, like pointing fingers. From one of these barges came float-ing up to me the sounds of a liquid voice, and a fire was burning in it, throwing a long red light that danced and quivered on the water. Here and there, both on the river and in the fields, other lights were glimmering, whether close at hand or far away, the eye could not dis-tinguish; they shrank together, then suddenly lengthened out into great blurs of light; grass-hoppers innumerable kept up an unceasing churr, persistent as the frogs of the Pontine marshes; and across the cloudless, but dark lowering sky floated from time to time the cries of unseen birds.

'Are we in Russia?' I asked of Alice.

'It is the Volga,' she answered.

We flew along the river-bank. 'Why did

you tear me away from there, from that lovely country?' I began. 'Were you envious, or was it jealousy in you?'

The lips of Alice faintly stirred, and again there was a menacing light in her eyes. . . . But her whole face grew stony again at once.

'I want to go home,' I said.

'Wait a little, wait a little,' answered Alice. 'To-night is a great night. It will not soon return. You may be a spectator. . . . Wait a little.'

And we suddenly flew across the Volga in a slanting direction, keeping close to the water's surface, with the low impetuous flight of swallows before a storm. The broad waves murmured heavily below us, the sharp river breeze beat upon us with its strong cold wing . . . the high right bank began soon to rise lip before us in the half-darkness. Steep mountains appeared with great ravines between. We came near to them.

'Shout: "Lads, to the barges!"' Alice whispered to me. I remembered the terror I had suffered at the apparition of the Roman phantoms. I felt weary and strangely heavy, as though my heart were ebbing away within me. I wished not to utter the fatal words; I knew beforehand that in response to them there would appear, as in the wolves' valley of the

Freischütz, some monstrous thing; but my lips parted against my will, and in a weak forced voice I shouted, also against my will: 'Lads, to the barges!'

XVI

AT first all was silence, even as it was at the Roman ruins, but suddenly I heard close to my very ear a coarse bargeman's laugh, and with a moan something dropped into the water and a gurgling sound followed. . . . I looked round: no one was anywhere to be seen, but from the bank the echo came bounding back, and at once from all sides rose a deafening din. There was a medley of everything in this chaos of sound: shouting and whining, furious abuse and laughter, laughter above everything; the plash of oars and the cleaving of hatchets, a crash as of the smashing of doors and chests, the grating of rigging and wheels, and the neighing of horses, and the clang of the alarm bell and the clink of chains, the roar and crackle of fire, drunken songs and quick, gnashing chatter, weeping inconsolable, plaintive despairing prayers, and shouts of command, the dying gasp and the reckless whistle, the guffaw and the thud of the dance . . . 'Kill

them! Hang them! Drown them! rip them
up! bravo! bravo! don't spare them!' could be
heard distinctly; I could even hear the hurried
breathing of men panting. And meanwhile all
around, as far as the eye could reach, nothing
could be seen, nothing was changed; the river
rolled by mysteriously, almost sullenly, the
very bank seemed more deserted and desolate
—and that was all.

I turned to Alice, but she put her finger to
her lips. . . .

'Stepan Timofeitch! Stepan Timofeitch is
coming!' was shouted noisily all round; 'he is
coming, our father, our ataman, our bread-
giver!' As before I saw nothing but it seemed
to me as though a huge body were moving
straight at me. . . .' Frolka! where art thou,
dog?' thundered an awful voice. 'Set fire to
every corner at once—and to the hatchet with
them, the white-handed scoundrels!'

I felt the hot breath of the flame close by,
and tasted the bitter savour of the smoke; and
at the same instant something warm like blood
spurted over my face and hands. . . . A savage
roar of laughter broke out all round. . . .

I lost consciousness, and when I came to
myself, Alice and I were gliding along beside
the familiar bushes that bordered my wood,
straight towards the old oak. . . .

'Do you see the little path?' Alice said to me, 'where the moon shines dimly and where are two birch-trees overhanging? Will you go there?'

But I felt so shattered and exhausted that I could only say in reply: 'Home! home!'

'You are at home,' replied Alice.

I was in fact standing at the very door of my house—alone. Alice had vanished. The yard-dog was about to approach, he scanned me suspiciously—and with a bark ran away.

With difficulty I dragged myself up to my bed and fell asleep without undressing.

XVII

ALL the following morning my head ached, and I could scarcely move my legs; but I cared little for my bodily discomfort; I was devoured by regret, overwhelmed with vexation.

I was excessively annoyed with myself. 'Coward!' I repeated incessantly; 'yes—Alice was right. What was I frightened of? how could I miss such an opportunity? . . . I might have seen Cæsar himself—and I was senseless with terror, I whimpered and turned away, like a child at the sight of the rod. Razin, now—

that's another matter. As a nobleman and landowner . . . though, indeed, even then what had I really to fear? Coward! coward!' . . .

'But wasn't it all a dream?' I asked myself at last. I called my housekeeper.

'Marfa, what o'clock did I go to bed yesterday—do you remember?'

'Why, who can tell, master? . . . Late enough, surely. Before it was quite dark you went out of the house; and you were tramping about in your bedroom when the night was more than half over. Just on morning—yes. And this is the third day it's been the same. You've something on your mind, it's easy to see.'

'Aha-ha!' I thought. 'Then there's no doubt about the flying. Well, and how do I look to-day?' I added aloud.

'How do you look? Let me have a look at you. You've got thinner a bit. Yes, and you're pale, master; to be sure, there's not a drop of blood in your face.'

I felt a slight twinge of uneasiness . . . I dismissed Marfa.

'Why, going on like this, you'll die, or go out of your mind, perhaps,' I reasoned with myself, as I sat deep in thought at the window. 'I must give it all up. It's dangerous And now my heart beats so strangely. And when I fly, I keep feeling as though some one were sucking at it, or as it were drawing something out of it—as the spring sap is drawn out of the birch-tree, if you stick an axe into it I 'm sorry, though. And Alice too. . . . She is playing cat and mouse with me . . . still she can hardly wish me harm. I will give myself up to her for the last time—and then. . . . But if she is drinking my blood? That's awful. Besides, such rapid locomotion cannot fail to be injurious; even in England, I'm told, on the railways, it 's against the law to go more than one hundred miles an hour. . . .'

So I reasoned with myself—but at ten o'clock in the evening, I was already at my post before the old oak-tree.

XVIII

THE night was cold, dull, grey; there was a feeling of rain in the air. To my amazement, I found no one under the oak; I walked several times round it, went up to the edge of the wood, turned back again, peered anxiously into the darkness. . . . All was emptiness. I waited a little, then several times I uttered the name, Alice, each time a little louder, . . . but she did not appear. I felt sad, almost sick at

138

heart; my previous apprehensions vanished; I could not resign myself to the idea that my companion would not come back to me again.

'Alice! Alice! come! Can it be you will not come?' I shouted, for the last time.

A crow, who had been waked by my voice, suddenly darted upwards into a tree-top close by, and catching in the twigs, fluttered his wings. . . . But Alice did not appear.

With downcast head, I turned homewards. Already I could discern the black outlines of the willows on the pond's edge, and the light in my window peeped out at me through the apple-trees in the orchard—peeped at me, and hid again, like the eye of some man keeping watch on me—when suddenly I heard behind me the faint swish of the rapidly parted air, and something at once embraced and snatched me upward, as a buzzard pounces on and snatches up a quail. . . . It was Alice sweeping down upon me. I felt her cheek against my cheek, her enfolding arm about my body, and like a cutting cold her whisper pierced to my ear, 'Here I am.' I was frightened and delighted both at once. . . . We flew at no great height above the ground.

'You did not mean to come to-day?' I said.

'And you were dull without me? You love me? Oh, you are mine!'

The last words of Alice confused me. . . . I did not know what to say.

'I was kept,' she went on; 'I was watched.'

'Who could keep you?'

'Where would you like to go?' inquired Alice, as usual not answering my question.

'Take me to Italy—to that lake, you remember.'

Alice turned a little away, and shook her head in refusal. At that point I noticed for the first time that she had ceased to be transparent. And her face seemed tinged with colour; there was a faint glow of red over its misty whiteness. I glanced at her eyes . . . and felt a pang of dread; in those eyes something was astir—with the slow, continuous, malignant movement of the benumbed snake, twisting and turning as the sun begins to thaw it.

'Alice,' I cried, 'who are you? Tell me who you are.'

Alice simply shrugged her shoulders.

I felt angry . . . I longed to punish her; and suddenly the idea occurred to me to tell her to fly with me to Paris. 'That's the place for you to be jealous,' I thought. 'Alice,' I said aloud, 'you are not afraid of big towns—Paris, for instance?'

'No.'

'Not even those parts where it is as light as in the boulevards?'

'It is not the light of day.'

'Good; then take me at once to the Boulevard des Italiens.'

Alice wrapped the end of her long hanging sleeve about my head. I was at once enfolded in a sort of white vapour full of the drowsy fragrance of the poppy. Everything disappeared at once; every light, every sound, and almost consciousness itself. Only the sense of being alive remained, and that was not unpleasant.

Suddenly the vapour vanished; Alice took her sleeve from my head, and I saw at my feet a huge mass of closely-packed buildings, brilliant light, movement, noisy traffic. . . . I saw Paris.

XIX

I HAD been in Paris before, and so I recognised at once the place to which Alice had directed her course. It was the Garden of the Tuileries with its old chestnut-trees, its iron railings, its fortress moat, and its brutal-looking Zouave sentinels. Passing the palace, passing the Church of St. Roche, on the steps of which the first Napoleon for the first time shed French blood, we came to a halt high over the Boulevard des Italiens, where the third Napoleon did the same thing and with the same success. Crowds of people, dandies young and old, workmen in blouses, women in gaudy dresses, were thronging on the pavements; the gilded restaurants and cafés were flaring with lights; omnibuses, carriages of all sorts and shapes, moved to and fro along the boulevard; everything was bustle, everything was brightness, wherever one chanced to look. . . . But, strange to say, I had no inclination to forsake my pure dark airy height. I had no inclination to get nearer to this human ant-hill. It seemed as though a hot, heavy, reddish vapour rose from it, half-fragrance, half-stench; so many lives were flung struggling in one heap together there. I was hesitating. . . . But suddenly, sharp as the clang of iron bars, the voice of a harlot of the streets floated up to me; like an insolent tongue, it was thrust out, this voice; it stung me like the sting of a viper. At once I saw in imagination the strong, heavy-jawed, greedy, flat Parisian face, the mercenary eyes, the paint and powder, the frizzed hair, and the nosegay of gaudy artificial flowers under the high-pointed hat, the polished nails like talons, the hideous crinoline. . . . I could fancy too one of our sons of the steppes running with pitiful eagerness after the doll put up for

sale. . . . I could fancy him with clumsy coarse-
ness and violent stammering, trying to imitate
the manners of the waiters at Véfour's, mincing,
flattering, wheedling . . . and a feeling of
loathing gained possession of me. . . . 'No,'
I thought, 'here Alice has no need to be
jealous. . . .'

Meanwhile I perceived that we had gradually
begun to descend. . . . Paris was rising to meet
us with all its din and odour. . . .

'Stop,' I said to Alice. 'Are you not stifled
and oppressed here?'

'You asked me to bring you here yourself.'

'I am to blame, I take back my word. Take
me away, Alice, I beseech you. To be sure,
here is Prince Kulmametov hobbling along the
boulevard; and his friend, Serge Varaksin,
waves his hand to him, shouting: "Ivan Stepa-
nitch, *allons souper*, make haste, zhay angazha
Rigol-bouche itself!" Take me away from
these furnished apartments and *maisons dorées*,
from the Jockey Club and the Figaro, from
close-shaven military heads and varnished bar-
racks, from sergents-de-ville with Napoleonic
beards, and from glasses of muddy absinthe,
from gamblers playing dominoes at the cafés,
and gamblers on the Bourse, from red ribbons
in button-holes, from M. de Four, inventor of
'matrimonial specialities,' and the gratuitous

143

consultations of Dr. Charles Albert, from liberal lectures and government pamphlets, from Parisian comedies and Parisian operas, from Parisian wit and Parisian ignorance. . . . Away! away! away!'

'Look down,' Alice answered; 'you are not now in Paris.'

I lowered my eyes. . . . It was true. A dark plain, intersected here and there by the whitish lines of roads, was rushing rapidly by below us, and only behind us on the horizon, like the reflection of an immense conflagration, rose the great glow of the innumerable lights of the capital of the world.

XX

AGAIN a veil fell over my eyes. . . . Again I lost consciousness. The veil was withdrawn at last What was it down there below? What was this park, with avenues of lopped lime-trees, with isolated fir-trees of the shape of parasols, with porticoes and temples in the Pompadour style, with statues of satyrs and nymphs of the Bernini school, with rococo tritons in the midst of meandering lakes, closed in by low parapets of blackened marble?

Wasn't it Versailles? No, it was not Versailles. A small palace, also rococo, peeped out behind a clump of bushy oaks. The moon shone dimly, shrouded in mist, and over the earth there was, as it were spread out, a delicate smoke. The eye could not decide what it was, whether moonlight or fog. On one of the lakes a swan was asleep; its long back was white as the snow of the frost-bound steppes, while glow-worms gleamed like diamonds in the bluish shadow at the base of a statue.

'We are near Mannheim,' said Alice; 'this is the Schwetzingen garden.'

'We are in Germany,' I thought, and I fell to listening. All was silence, except somewhere, secluded and unseen, the splash and babble of falling water. It seemed continually to repeat the same words: 'Aye, aye, aye, for aye, aye.' And all at once I fancied that in the very centre of one of the avenues, between clipped walls of green, a cavalier came tripping along in red-heeled boots, a gold-braided coat, with lace ruffs at his wrists, a light steel rapier at his thigh, smilingly offering his arm to a lady in a powdered wig and a gay chintz. . . . Strange, pale faces. . . . I tried to look into them. . . . But already everything had vanished, and as before there was nothing but the babbling water.

'Those are dreams wandering,' whispered Alice; 'yesterday there was much—oh, much—to see; to-day, even the dreams avoid man's eye. Forward! forward!'

We soared higher and flew farther on. So smooth and easy was our flight that it seemed that we moved not, but everything moved to meet us. Mountains came into view, dark, undulating, covered with forest; they rose up and swam towards us. . . . And now they were slipping by beneath us, with all their windings, hollows, and narrow glades, with gleams of light from rapid brooks among the slumbering trees at the bottom of the dales; and in front of us more mountains sprung up again and floated towards us. . . . We were in the heart of the Black Forest.

Mountains, still mountains . . . and forest, magnificent, ancient, stately forest. The night sky was clear; I could recognise some kinds of trees, especially the splendid firs, with their straight white trunks. Here and there on the edge of the forest, wild goats could be seen; graceful and alert, they stood on their slender legs and listened, turning their heads prettily and pricking up their great funnel-shaped ears. A ruined tower, sightless and gloomy, on the crest of a bare cliff, laid bare its crumbling turrets; above the old forgotten stones, a little golden star was shining peacefully. From a small almost black lake rose, like a mysterious wail, the plaintive croak of tiny frogs. I fancied other notes, long-drawn-out, languid like the strains of an Æolian harp. . . . Here we were in the home of legend! The same delicate moonlight mist, which had struck me in Schwetzingen, was shed here on every side, and the farther away the mountains, the thicker was this mist. I counted up five, six, ten different tones of shadow at different heights on the mountain slopes, and over all this realm of varied silence the moon queened it pensively. The air blew in soft, light currents. I felt myself a lightness at heart, and, as it were, a lofty calm and melancholy. . . .

'Alice, you must love this country!'

'I love nothing.'

'How so? Not me?'

'Yes . . . you!' she answered indifferently.

It seemed to me that her arm clasped my waist more tightly than before.

'Forward! forward!' said Alice, with a sort of cold fervour.

'Forward!' I repeated

XXI

A LOUD, thrilling cry rang out suddenly over our heads, and was at once repeated a little in front.

'Those are belated cranes flying to you, to the north,' said Alice; 'would you like to join them?'

'Yes, yes! raise me up to them.'

We darted upwards and in one instant found ourselves beside the flying flock.

The big handsome birds (there were thirteen of them) were flying in a triangle, with slow sharp flaps of their hollow wings; with their heads and legs stretched rigidly out, and their breasts stiffly pressed forward, they pushed on persistently and so swiftly that the air whistled about them. It was marvellous at such a height, so remote from all things living, to see such passionate, strenuous life, such unflinching will, untiringly cleaving their triumphant way through space. The cranes now and then called to one another, the foremost to the hindmost; and there was a certain pride, dignity, and invincible faith in these loud cries, this converse in the clouds. 'We shall get there, be sure, hard though it be,' they seemed to say, cheering one another on. And then the thought came to me that men, such as these birds—in Russia —nay, in the whole world, are few.

'We are flying towards Russia now,' observed Alice. I noticed now, not for the first time, that she almost always knew what I was thinking of. 'Would you like to go back?'

'Let us go back . . . or no! I have been in Paris; take me to Petersburg.'

'Now?'

'At once. . . . Only wrap my head in your veil, or it will go ill with me.'

Alice raised her hand . . . but before the mist enfolded me, I had time to feel on my lips the contact of that soft, dull sting. . . .

XXII

'Li-i-isten!' sounded in my ears a long drawn out cry. 'Li-i-isten!' was echoed back with a sort of desperation in the distance. 'Li-i-isten!' died away somewhere far, far away. I started. A tall golden spire flashed on my eyes; I recognised the fortress of St. Peter and St. Paul.

A northern, pale night! But was it night at all? Was it not rather a pallid, sickly daylight? I never liked Petersburg nights; but this time the night seemed even fearful to me; the face of Alice had vanished completely, melted away like the mist of morning in the July sun, and I saw her whole body clearly, as it hung, heavy and solitary on a level with the Alexander column. So here was Petersburg! Yes, it was Petersburg, no doubt. The wide empty grey streets; the greyish-white, and yellowish-grey and greyish-lilac houses, covered with stucco, which was peeling off, with their sunken windows, gaudy sign-boards, iron canopies over steps, and wretched little greengrocer's shops; the façades, inscriptions, sentry-boxes, troughs; the golden cap of St. Isaac's; the senseless motley Bourse; the granite walls of the fortress, and the broken wooden pavement; the barges loaded with hay and timber; the smell of dust, cabbage, matting, and hemp; the stony-faced dvorniks in sheep-skin coats, with high collars; the cab-drivers, huddled up dead asleep on their decrepit cabs —yes, this was Petersburg, our northern Palmyra. Everything was visible; everything was clear—cruelly clear and distinct—and everything was mournfully sleeping, standing out in strange huddled masses in the dull clear air. The flush of sunset—a hectic flush—had not yet gone, and would not be gone till morning from the white starless sky; it was reflected on the silken surface of the Neva, while faintly gurgling and faintly moving, the cold blue waves hurried on. . . .

'Let us fly away,' Alice implored.

And without waiting for my reply, she bore me away across the Neva, over the palace square to Liteiny Street. Steps and voices were audible beneath us; a group of young men, with worn faces, came along the street talking about dancing-classes. 'Sub-lieutenant Stolpakov's seventh!' shouted suddenly a soldier, standing half-asleep on guard at a pyramid of rusty bullets; and a little farther on, at an open window in a tall house, I saw a girl in a creased silk dress, without cuffs, with a pearl net on her hair, and a cigarette in her mouth. She was reading a book with reverent attention; it was a volume of the works of one of our modern Juvenals.

'Let us fly away!' I said to Alice.

One instant more, and there were glimpses below us of the rotting pine copses and mossy bogs surrounding Petersburg. We bent our course straight to the south; sky, earth, all grew gradually darker and darker. The sick night; the sick daylight; the sick town—all were left behind us.

XXIII

WE flew more slowly than usual, and I was able to follow with my eyes the immense expanse of my native land gradually unfolding before me, like the unrolling of an endless panorama. Forests, copses, fields, ravines, rivers—here and there villages and churches—and again fields and forests and copses and ravines. . . . Sadness came over me, and a kind of indifferent dreariness. And I was not sad and dreary simply because it was Russia I was flying over. No. The earth itself, this flat surface which lay spread out beneath me; the whole earthly globe, with its populations, multitudinous, feeble, crushed by want, grief and diseases, bound to a clod of pitiful dust; this brittle, rough crust, this shell over the fiery sands of our planet, overspread with the mildew we call the organic, vegetable kingdom; these human flies, a thousand times paltrier than flies; their dwellings glued together with filth, the pitiful traces of their tiny, monotonous bustle, of their comic struggle with the unchanging and inevitable, how revolting it all suddenly was to me. My heart turned slowly sick, and I could not bear to gaze longer on these trivial pictures, on this vulgar show. . . . Yes, I felt dreary, worse than dreary. Even pity I felt nothing of for my brother men: all feelings in me were merged in one which I scarcely dare to name: a feeling of loathing, and stronger than all and more than all within me was the loathing—for myself.

'Cease,' whispered Alice, 'cease, or I cannot carry you. You have grown heavy.'

'Home,' I answered her in the very tone in which I used to say the word to my coachman, when I came out at four o'clock at night from some Moscow friends', where I had been talking since dinner-time of the future of Russia and the significance of the commune. 'Home,' I repeated, and closed my eyes.

XXIV

But I soon opened them again. Alice seemed huddling strangely up to me; she was almost pushing against me. I looked at her and my blood froze at the sight. One who has chanced to behold on the face of another a sudden look of intense terror, the cause of which he does not suspect, will understand me. By terror, overmastering terror, the pale features of Alice were drawn and contorted, almost effaced. I had never seen anything like it even on a

153

living human face. A lifeless, misty phantom, a shade, . . . and this deadly horror. . . .

'Alice, what is it? I said at last.

'She . . . she . . .' she answered with an effort. 'She.'

'She? Who is she?'

'Do not utter her name, not her name, Alice faltered hurriedly.' We must escape, or there will be an end to everything, and for ever . . . Look, over there!'

I turned my head in the direction in which her trembling hand was pointing, and discerned something . . . something horrible indeed.

This something was the more horrible that it had no definite shape. Something bulky, dark, yellowish-black, spotted like a lizard's belly, not a storm-cloud, and not smoke, was crawling with a snake-like motion over the earth. A wide rhythmic undulating movement from above downwards, and from below upwards, an undulation recalling the malignant sweep of the wings of a vulture seeking its prey; at times an indescribably revolting grovelling on the earth, as of a spider stooping over its captured fly. . . . Who are you, what are you, menacing mass? Under her influence, I saw it, I felt it —all sank into nothingness, all was dumb. . . . A putrefying, pestilential chill came from it. At this chill breath the heart turned sick, and the eyes grew dim, and the hair stood up on the head. It was a power moving; that power which there is no resisting, to which all is subject, which, sightless, shapeless, senseless, sees all, knows all, and like a bird of prey picks out its victims, like a snake, stifles them and stabs them with its frozen sting. . . .

'Alice! Alice!' I shrieked like one in frenzy. 'It is death! death itself!'

The wailing sound I had heard before broke from Alice's lips; this time it was more like a human wail of despair, and we flew. But our flight was strangely and alarmingly unsteady; Alice turned over in the air, fell, rushed from side to side like a partridge mortally wounded, or trying to attract a dog away from her young. And meanwhile in pursuit of us, parting from the indescribable mass of horror, rushed sort of long undulating tentacles, like outstretched arms, like talons. . . . Suddenly a huge shape, a muffled figure on a pale horse, sprang up and flew upwards into the very heavens. . . . Still more fearfully, still more desperately Alice struggled. 'She has seen! All is over! I am lost!' I heard her broken whisper. 'Oh, I am miserable! I might have profited, have won life, . . . and now. . . . Nothingness, nothingness!' It was too unbearable. . . . I lost consciousness.

XXV

WHEN I came to myself, I was lying on my back in the grass, feeling a dull ache all over me, as from a bad bruise. The dawn was beginning in the sky: I could clearly distinguish things. Not far off, alongside a birch copse, ran a road planted with willows: the country seemed familiar to me. I began to recollect what had happened to me, and shuddered all over directly my mind recalled the last, hideous apparition. . . .

'But what was Alice afraid of?' I thought. 'Can she too be subject to that power? Is she not immortal? Can she too be in danger of annihilation, dissolution? How is it possible?'

A soft moan sounded close by me. I turned my head. Two paces from me lay stretched out motionless a young woman in a white gown, with thick disordered tresses, with bare shoulders. One arm was thrown behind her head, the other had fallen on her bosom. Her eyes were closed, and on her tightly shut lips stood a fleck of crimson stain. Could it be Alice? But Alice was a phantom, and I was looking upon a living woman. I crept up to her, bent down. . . .

'Alice, is it you?' I cried. Suddenly, slowly

quivering, the wide eyelids rose; dark piercing eyes were fastened upon me, and at the same instant lips too fastened upon me, warm, moist, smelling of blood . . . soft arms twined tightly round my neck, a burning, full heart pressed convulsively to mine. 'Farewell, farewell for ever!' the dying voice uttered distinctly, and everything vanished.

I got up, staggering like a drunken man, and passing my hands several times over my face, looked carefully about me. I found myself near the high road, a mile and a half from my own place. The sun had just risen when I got home.

All the following nights I awaited—and I confess not without alarm—the appearance of my phantom; but it did not visit me again. I even set off one day, in the dusk, to the old oak, but nothing took place there out of the common. I did not, however, overmuch regret the discontinuance of this strange acquaintance. I reflected much and long over this inexplicable, almost unintelligible phenomenon; and I am convinced that not only science cannot explain it, but that even in fairy tales and legends nothing like it is to be met with. What was Alice, after all? An apparition, a restless soul, an evil spirit, a sylphide, a vampire, or what? Sometimes it struck me again that Alice was a woman I had known at some time or other, and I made tremendous efforts to recall where I had seen her. . . . Yes, yes, I thought sometimes, directly, this minute, I shall remember. . . . In a flash everything had melted away again like a dream. Yes, I thought a great deal, and, as is always the way, came to no conclusion. The advice or opinion of others I could not bring myself to invite; fearing to be taken for a madman. I gave up all reflection upon it at last; to tell the truth, I had no time for it. For one thing, the emancipation had come along with the redistribution of property, etc.; and for another, my own health failed; I suffered with my chest, with sleeplessness, and a cough. I got thin all over. My face was yellow as a dead man's. The doctor declares I have too little blood, calls my illness by the Greek name, 'anæmia,' and is sending me to Gastein. The arbitrator swears that without me there's no coming to an understanding with the peasants. Well, what's one to do?

But what is the meaning of the piercingly-pure, shrill notes, the notes of an harmonica, which I hear directly any one's death is spoken of before me? They keep growing louder, more penetrating. . . . And why do I shudder in such anguish at the mere thought of annihilation?

THE SONG
OF TRIUMPHANT LOVE

[MDXLII]

DEDICATED
TO THE MEMORY OF GUSTAVE FLAUBERT

'Wage Du su irren und zu träumen!' —Schiller

THE SONG
OF TRIUMPHANT LOVE

THIS is what I read in an old Italian manuscript:—

I

About the middle of the sixteenth century
there were living in Ferrara (it was at that
time flourishing under the sceptre of its magnificent archdukes, the patrons of the arts and
poetry) two young men, named Fabio and
Muzzio. They were of the same age, and of
near kinship, and were scarcely ever apart; the
warmest affection had united them from early
childhood . . . the similarity of their positions
strengthened the bond. Both belonged to old
families; both were rich, independent, and
without family ties; tastes and inclinations
were alike in both. Muzzio was devoted to
music, Fabio to painting. They were looked
upon with pride by the whole of Ferrara, as

ornaments of the court, society, and town. In appearance, however, they were not alike, though both were distinguished by a graceful, youthful beauty. Fabio was taller, fair of face and flaxen of hair, and he had blue eyes. Muzzio, on the other hand, had a swarthy face and black hair, and in his dark brown eyes there was not the merry light, nor on his lips the genial smile of Fabio; his thick eyebrows overhung narrow eyelids, while Fabio's golden eyebrows formed delicate half-circles on his pure, smooth brow. In conversation, too, Muzzio was less animated. For all that, the two friends were both alike looked on with favour by ladies, as well they might be, being models of chivalrous courtliness and generosity.

At the same time there was living in Ferrara a girl named Valeria. She was considered one of the greatest beauties in the town, though it was very seldom possible to see her, as she led a retired life, and never went out except to church, and on great holidays for a walk. She lived with her mother, a widow of noble family, though of small fortune, who had no other children. In every one whom Valeria met she inspired a sensation of involuntary admiration, and an equally involuntary tenderness and respect, so modest was her mien, so little, it seemed, was she aware of all the power of her

own charms. Some, it is true, found her a
little pale; her eyes, almost always downcast,
expressed a certain shyness, even timidity; her
lips rarely smiled, and then only faintly; her
voice scarcely any one had heard. But the
rumour went that it was most beautiful, and
that, shut up in her own room, in the early
morning when everything still slumbered in the
town, she loved to sing old songs to the sound
of the lute, on which she used to play herself.
In spite of her pallor, Valeria was blooming
with health; and even old people, as they
gazed on her, could not but think, Oh, how
happy the youth for whom that pure maiden
bud, still enfolded in its petals, will one day
open into full flower!'

II

FABIO and Muzzio saw Valeria for the first
time at a magnificent public festival, celebrated
at the command of the Archduke of Ferrara,
Ercol, son of the celebrated Lucrezia Borgia, in
honour of some illustrious grandees who had
come from Paris on the invitation of the
Archduchess, daughter of the French king
Louis XII. Valeria was sitting beside her

mother on an elegant tribune, built after a design of Palladio, in the principal square of Ferrara, for the most honourable ladies in the town. Both Fabio and Muzzio fell passionately in love with her on that day; and, as they never had any secrets from each other, each of them soon knew what was passing in his friend's heart. They agreed together that both should try to get to know Valeria; and if she should deign to choose one of them, the other should submit without a murmur to her decision. A few weeks later, thanks to the excellent renown they deservedly enjoyed, they succeeded in penetrating into the widow's house, difficult though it was to obtain an entry to it; she permitted them to visit her. From that time forward they were able almost every day to see Valeria and to converse with her; and every day the passion kindled in the hearts of both young men grew stronger and stronger. Valeria, however, showed no preference for either of them, though their society was obviously agreeable to her. With Muzzio, she occupied herself with music; but she talked more with Fabio, with him she was less timid. At last, they resolved to learn once for all their fate, and sent a letter to Valeria, in which they begged her to be open with them, and to say to which she would be ready to give her hand.

Valeria showed this letter to her mother, and declared that she was willing to remain un- married, but if her mother considered it time for her to enter upon matrimony, then she would marry whichever one her mother's choice should fix upon. The excellent widow shed a few tears at the thought of parting from her beloved child; there was, however, no good ground for refusing the suitors, she considered both of them equally worthy of her daughter's hand. But, as she secretly preferred Fabio, and suspected that Valeria liked him the better, she fixed upon him. The next day Fabio heard of his happy fate, while all that was left for Muzzio was to keep his word, and submit.

And this he did; but to be the witness of the triumph of his friend and rival was more than he could do. He promptly sold the greater part of his property, and collecting some thousands of ducats, he set off on a far journey to the East. As he said farewell to Fabio, he told him that he should not return till he felt that the last traces of passion had vanished from his heart. It was painful to Fabio to part from the friend of his childhood and youth . . . but the joyous anticipation of approaching bliss soon swallowed up all other sensations, and he gave himself up wholly to the transports of successful love.

Shortly after, he celebrated his nuptials with Valeria, and only then learnt the full worth of the treasure it had been his fortune to obtain. He had a charming villa, shut in by a shady garden, a short distance from Ferrara; he moved thither with his wife and her mother. Then a time of happiness began for them. Married life brought out in a new and enchanting light all the perfections of Valeria. Fabio became an artist of distinction—no longer a mere amateur, but a real master. Valeria's mother rejoiced, and thanked God as she looked upon the happy pair. Four years flew by un perceived, like a delicious dream. One thing only was wanting to the young couple, one lack they mourned over as a sorrow: they had no children . . . but they had not given up all hope of them. At the end of the fourth year they were overtaken by a great, this time a real sorrow; Valeria's mother died after an illness of a few days.

Many tears were shed by Valeria; for a long time she could not accustom herself to her loss. But another year went by; life again asserted its rights and flowed along its old channel. And behold, one fine summer evening, unexpected by every one, Muzzio returned to Ferrara.

III

DURING the whole space of five years that had
elapsed since his departure no one had heard
anything of him; all talk about him had died
away, as though he had vanished from the face
of the earth. When Fabio met his friend in
one of the streets of Ferrara he almost cried out
aloud, first in alarm and then in delight, and
he at once invited him to his villa. There
happened to be in his garden there a spacious
pavilion, apart from the house; he proposed to
his friend that he should establish himself in
this pavilion. Muzzio readily agreed and moved
thither the same day together with his servant,
a dumb Malay—dumb but not deaf, and indeed,
to judge by the alertness of his expression, a
very intelligent man. . . . His tongue had been
cut out. Muzzio brought with him dozens of
boxes, filled with treasures of all sorts collected
by him in the course of his prolonged travels.
Valeria was delighted at Muzzio's return; and
he greeted her with cheerful friendliness, but
composure; it could be seen in every action
that he had kept the promise given to Fabio.
During the day he completely arranged everything in order in his pavilion; aided by his

Malay, he unpacked the curiosities he had
brought; rugs, silken stuffs, velvet and brocaded
garments, weapons, goblets, dishes and bowls,
decorated with enamel, things made of gold
and silver, and inlaid with pearl and turquoise,
carved boxes of jasper and ivory, cut bottles,
spices, incense, skins of wild beasts, and
feathers of unknown birds, and a number of
other things, the very use of which seemed mysterious and incomprehensible. Among all these
precious things there was a rich pearl necklace,
bestowed upon Muzzio by the king of Persia
for some great and secret service; he asked
permission of Valeria to put this necklace with
his own hand about her neck; she was struck
by its great weight and a sort of strange heat
in it . . . it seemed to burn to her skin. In
the evening after dinner as they sat on the
terrace of the villa in the shade of the oleanders
and laurels, Muzzio began to relate his adventures. He told of the distant lands he had
seen, of cloud-topped mountains and deserts,
rivers like seas; he told of immense buildings
and temples, of trees a thousand years old, of
birds and flowers of the colours of the rainbow:
he named the cities and the peoples he had
visited . . . their very names seemed like a fairy
tale. The whole East was familiar to Muzzio;
he had traversed Persia, Arabia, where the

horses are nobler and more beautiful than any other living creatures; he had penetrated into the very heart of India, where the race of men grow like stately trees; he had reached the boundaries of China and Thibet, where the living god, called the Grand Llama, dwells on earth in the guise of a silent man with narrow eyes. Marvellous were his tales. Both Fabio and Valeria listened to him as if enchanted. Muzzio's features had really changed very little; his face, swarthy from childhood, had grown darker still, burnt under the rays of a hotter sun, his eyes seemed more deep-set than-before —and that was all; but the expression of his face had become different: concentrated and dignified, it never showed more life when he recalled the dangers he had encountered by night in forests that resounded with the roar of tigers or by day on solitary ways where savage fanatics lay in wait for travellers, to slay them in honour of their iron goddess who demands human sacrifices. And Muzzio's voice had grown deeper and more even; his hands, his whole body had lost the freedom of gesture peculiar to the Italian race. With the aid of his servant, the obsequiously alert Malay, he showed his hosts a few of the feats he had learnt from the Indian Brahmins. Thus for instance, having first hidden himself behind a curtain, he suddenly appeared sitting in the air cross-legged, the tips of his fingers pressed lightly on a bamboo cane placed vertically, which astounded Fabio not a little and positively alarmed Valeria. . . . 'Isn't he a sorcerer?' was her thought. When he proceeded, piping on a little flute, to call some tame snakes out of a covered basket, where their dark flat heads with quivering tongues appeared under a particoloured cloth, Valeria was terrified and begged Muzzio to put away these loathsome horrors as soon as possible. At supper Muzzio regaled his friends with wine of Shiraz from a round long-necked flagon; it was of extraordinary fragrance and thickness, of a golden colour with a shade of green in it, and it shone with a strange brightness as it was poured into the tiny jasper goblets. In taste it was unlike European wines: it was very sweet and spicy, and, drunk slowly in small draughts, produced a sensation of pleasant drowsiness in all the limbs. Muzzio made both Fabio and Valeria drink a goblet of it, and he drank one himself. Bending over her goblet he murmured something, moving his fingers as he did so. Valeria noticed this; but as in all Muzzio's doings, in his whole behaviour, there was something strange and out of the common, she only thought, 'Can he have adopted some new faith in India, or is that the custom there?' Then after a short silence she asked him: 'Had he persevered with music during his travels? Muzzio, in reply, bade the Malay bring his Indian violin. It was like those of to-day, but instead of four strings it had only three, the upper part of it was covered with a bluish snake-skin, and the slender bow of reed was in the form of a half-moon, and on its extreme end glittered a pointed diamond.

Muzzio played first some mournful airs, national songs as he told them, strange and even barbarous to an Italian ear; the sound of the metallic strings was plaintive and feeble. But when Muzzio began the last song, it suddenly gained force and rang out tunefully and powerfully; the passionate melody flowed out under the wide sweeps of the bow, flowed out, exquisitely twisting and coiling like the snake that covered the violin-top; and such fire, such triumphant bliss glowed and burned in this melody that Fabio and Valeria felt wrung to the heart and tears came into their eyes; . . . while Muzzio, his head bent, and pressed close to the violin, his cheeks pale, his eyebrows drawn together into a single straight line, seemed still more concentrated and solemn; and the diamond at the end of the bow flashed sparks of light as though it too were kindled by the fire of the divine song. When Muzzio had finished, and still keeping fast the violin between his chin and his shoulder, dropped the hand that held the bow, 'What is that? What is that you have been playing to us?' cried Fabio. Valeria uttered not a word—but her whole being seemed echoing her husband's question. Muzzio laid the violin on the table—and slightly tossing back his hair, he said with a polite smile: 'That—that melody . . .that song I heard once in the island of Ceylon. That song is known there among the people as the song of happy, triumphant love.' 'Play it again,' Fabio was murmuring. 'No; it can't be played again,' answered Muzzio. 'Besides, it is now too late. Signora Valeria ought to be at rest; and it 's time for me too . . . I am weary.' During the whole day Muzzio had treated Valeria with respectful simplicity, as a friend of former days, but as he went out he clasped her hand very tightly, squeezing his fingers on her palm, and looking so intently into her face that though she did not raise her eyelids, she yet felt the look on her suddenly flaming cheeks. She said nothing to Muzzio, but jerked away her hand, and when he was gone, she gazed at the door through which he had passed out. She remembered how she had been a little afraid of him even in old days . . .

and now she was overcome by perplexity. Muzzio went off to his pavilion: the husband and wife went to their bedroom.

IV

VALERIA did not quickly fall asleep; there was a faint and languid fever in her blood and a slight ringing in her ears . . . from that strange wine, as she supposed, and perhaps too from Muzzio's stories, from his playing on the violin . . . towards morning she did at last fall asleep, and she had an extraordinary dream.

She dreamt that she was going into a large room with a low ceiling . . . Such a room she had never seen in her life. All the walls were covered with tiny blue tiles with gold lines on them; slender carved pillars of alabaster supported the marble ceiling; the ceiling itself and the pillars seemed half transparent . . . a pale rosy light penetrated from all sides into the room, throwing a mysterious and uniform light on all the objects in it; brocaded cushions lay on a narrow rug in the very middle of the floor, which was smooth as a mirror. In the corners almost unseen were smoking lofty

173

censers, of the shape of monstrous beasts; there
was no window anywhere; a door hung with a
velvet curtain stood dark and silent in a recess
in the wall. And suddenly this curtain slowly
glided, moved aside . . . and in came Muzzio.
He bowed, opened his arms, laughed . . . His
fierce arms enfolded Valeria's waist; his
parched lips burned her all over. . . . She fell
backwards on the cushions.

.   .   .   .   .   .

Moaning with horror, after long struggles,
Valeria awaked. Still not realising where she
was and what was happening to her, she raised
herself on her bed, looked round . . . A tremor
ran over her whole body. . . . Fabio was lying
beside her. He was asleep; but his face in the
light of the brilliant full moon looking in at
the window was pale as a corpse's . . . it was
sadder than a dead face. Valeria waked her
husband, and directly he looked at her. 'What
is the matter?' he cried. 'I had—I had a
fearful dream,' she whispered, still shuddering
all over.

But at that instant from the direction of the
pavilion came floating powerful sounds, and
both Fabio and Valeria recognised the melody
Muzzio had played to them, calling it the song
of blissful triumphant love. Fabio looked in
perplexity at Valeria . . . she closed her eyes,

turned away, and both holding their breath, heard the song out to the end. As the last note died away, the moon passed behind a cloud, it was suddenly dark in the room. . . . Both the young people let their heads sink on their pillows without exchanging a word, and neither of them noticed when the other fell asleep.

V

THE next morning Muzzio came in to breakfast; he seemed happy and greeted Valeria cheerfully. She answered him in confusion— stole a glance at him—and felt frightened at the sight of that serene happy face, those piercing and inquisitive eyes. Muzzio was beginning again to tell some story . . . but Fabio interrupted him at the first word.

'You could not sleep, I see, in your new quarters. My wife and I heard you playing last night's song.'

'Yes! Did you hear it?' said Muzzio. 'I played it indeed; but I had been asleep before that, and I had a wonderful dream too.'

Valeria was on the alert. 'What sort of dream?' asked Fabio.

'I dreamed,' answered Muzzio, not taking his eyes off Valeria, 'I was entering a spacious apartment with a ceiling decorated in Oriental fashion, carved columns supported the roof, the walls were covered with tiles, and though there were neither windows nor lights, the whole room was filled with a rosy light, just as though it were all built of transparent stone. In the corners, Chinese censers were smoking, on the floor lay brocaded cushions along a narrow rug. I went in through a door covered with a curtain, and at another door just opposite appeared a woman whom I once loved. And so beautiful she seemed to me, that I was all aflame with my old love . . .'

Muzzio broke off significantly. Valeria sat motionless, and only gradually she turned white . . . and she drew her breath more slowly.

Then,' continued Muzzio, 'I waked up and played that song.'

'But who was that woman?' said Fabio.

'Who was she? The wife of an Indian—I met her in the town of Delhi . . . She is not alive now—she died.'

'And her husband?' asked Fabio, not knowing why he asked the question.

'Her husband, too, they say is dead. I soon lost sight of them both.'

'Strange!' observed Fabio. 'My wife too had an extraordinary dream last night'— Muzzio gazed intently at Valeria—'which she did not tell me,' added Fabio.

But at this point Valeria got up and went out of the room. Immediately after breakfast, Muzzio too went away, explaining that he had to be in Ferrara on business, and that he would not be back before the evening.

VI

A FEW weeks before Muzzio's return, Fabio had begun a portrait of his wife, depicting her with the attributes of Saint Cecilia. He had made considerable advance in nis art; the renowned Luini, a pupil of Leonardo da Vinci, used to come to him at Ferrara, and while aiding him with his own counsels, pass on also the precepts of his great master. The portrait was almost completely finished; all that was left was to add a few strokes to the face, and Fabio might well be proud of his creation. After seeing Muzzio off on his way to Ferrara, he turned into his studio, where Valeria was usually waiting for him; but he did not find

her there; he called her, she did not respond.
Fabio was overcome by a secret uneasiness; he
began looking for her. She was nowhere in the
house; Fabio ran into the garden, and there in
one of the more secluded walks he caught sight
of Valeria. She was sitting on a seat, her head
drooping on to her bosom and her hands folded
upon her knees; while behind her, peeping out
of the dark green of a cypress, a marble satyr,
with a distorted malignant grin on his face, was
putting his pouting lips to a Pan's pipe. Valeria
was visibly relieved at her husband's appearance,
and to his agitated questions she replied that
she had a slight headache, but that it was of no
consequence, and she was ready to come to sit
to him. Fabio led her to the studio, posed her,
and took up his brush; but to his great vexation, he could not finish the face as he would
have liked to. And not because it was somewhat pale and looked exhausted . . . no; but
the pure, saintly expression, which he liked so
much in it, and which had given him the idea
of painting Valeria as Saint Cecilia, he could
not find in it that day, He flung down the
brush at last, told his wife he was not in the
mood for work, and that he would not prevent
her from lying down, as she did not look at all
well, and put the canvas with its face to the
wall Valeria agreed with him that she ought

178

to rest, and repeating her complaints of a headache, withdrew into her bedroom.

Fabio remained in the studio. He felt a strange confused sensation incomprehensible to himself. Muzzio's stay under his roof, to which he, Fabio, had himself urgently invited him, was irksome to him. And not that he was jealous —could any one have been jealous of Valeria! —but he did not recognise his former comrade in his friend. All that was strange, unknown and new that Muzzio had brought with him from those distant lands—and which seemed to have entered into his very flesh and blood— all these magical feats, songs, strange drinks, this dumb Malay, even the spicy fragrance diffused by Muzzio's garments, his hair, his breath—all this inspired in Fabio a sensation akin to distrust, possibly even to timidity. And why did that Malay waiting at table stare with such disagreeable intentness at him, Fabio? Really any one might suppose that he understood Italian. Muzzio had said of him that in losing his tongue, this Malay had made a great sacrifice, and, in return he was now possessed of great power. What sort of power? and how could he have obtained it at the price of his tongue? All this was very strange! very incomprehensible! Fabio went into his wife's room; she was lying on the bed, dressed, but was not asleep. Hearing his steps, she started, then again seemed delighted to see him just as in the garden. Fabio sat down beside the bed, took Valeria by the hand, and after a short silence, asked her, 'What was the extraordinary dream that had frightened her so the previous night? And was it the same sort at all as the dream Muzzio had described?' Valeria crimsoned and said hurriedly: 'O! no! no! I saw . . . a sort of monster which was trying to tear me to pieces.' 'A monster? in the shape of a man?' asked Fabio. 'No, a beast . . . a beast!' Valeria turned away and hid her burning face in the pillows. Fabio held his wife's hand some time longer; silently he raised it to his lips, and withdrew.

Both the young people passed that day with heavy hearts. Something dark seemed hanging over their heads . . . but what it was, they could not tell. They wanted to be together, as though some danger threatened them; but what to say to one another they did not know. Fabio made an effort to take up the portrait, and to read Ariosto, whose poem had appeared not long before in Ferrara, and was now making a noise all over Italy; but nothing was of any use. . . . Late in the evening, just at supper-time, Muzzio returned.

VII

HE seemed composed and cheerful—but he told them little; he devoted himself rather to questioning Fabio about their common acquaintances, about the German war, and the Emperor Charles: he spoke of his own desire to visit Rome, to see the new Pope. He again offered Valeria some Shiraz wine, and on her refusal, observed as though to himself, 'Now it's not needed, to be sure.' Going back with his wife to their room, Fabio soon fell asleep; and waking up an hour later, felt a conviction that no one was sharing his bed; Valeria was not beside him. He got up quickly and at the same instant saw his wife in her night attire coming out of the garden into the room. The moon was shining brightly, though not long before a light rain had been falling. With eyes closed, with an expression of mysterious horror on her immovable face, Valeria approached the bed, and feeling for it with her hands stretched out before her, lay down hurriedly and in silence. Fabio turned to her with a question, but she made no reply; she seemed to be asleep. He touched her, and felt on her dress and on her hair drops of rain, and on the soles of her bare feet, little grains of sand. Then he leapt up and ran into the garden through the half-open door. The crude brilliance of the moon wrapt every object in light. Fabio looked about him, and perceived on the sand of the path prints of two pairs of feet—one pair were bare; and these prints led to a bower of jasmine, on one side, between the pavilion and the house. He stood still in perplexity, and suddenly once more he heard the strains of the song he had listened to the night before, Fabio shuddered, ran into the pavilion. . . . Muzzio was standing in the middle of the room playing on the violin. Fabio rushed up to him.

'You have been in the garden, your clothes are wet with rain.'

'No . . . I don't know . . . I think . . . I have not been out . . .' Muzzio answered slowly, seeming amazed at Fabio's entrance and his excitement.

Fabio seized him by the hand. 'And why are you playing that melody again? Have you had a dream again?'

Muzzio glanced at Fabio with the same look of amazement, and said nothing.

'Answer me!'

'"The moon stood high like a round shield . . .
Like a snake, the river shines..,
The friend's awake, the foe's asleep . . .
The bird is in the falcon's clutches . . . Help!"'

muttered Muzzio, humming to himself as though in delirium.

Fabio stepped back two paces, stared at Muzzio, pondered a moment . . . and went back to the house, to his bedroom.

Valeria, her head sunk on her shoulder and her hands hanging lifelessly, was in a heavy sleep. He could not quickly awaken her . . . but directly she saw him, she flung herself on his neck, and embraced him convulsively; she was trembling all over. 'What is the matter, my precious, what is it?' Fabio kept repeating, trying to soothe her. But she still lay lifeless on his breast. 'Ah, what fearful dreams I have!' she whispered, hiding her face against him. Fabio would have questioned her . . . but she only shuddered. The window-panes were flushed with the early light of morning when at last she fell asleep in his arms.

VIII

THE next day Muzzio disappeared from early morning, while Valeria informed her husband that she intended to go away to a neighbouring monastery, where lived her spiritual father, an old and austere monk, in whom she placed unbounded confidence. To Fabio's inquiries she replied, that she wanted by confession to relieve her soul, which was weighed down by the exceptional impressions of the last few days. As he looked upon Valeria's sunken face, and listened to her faint voice, Fabio approved of her plan; the worthy Father Lorenzo might give her valuable advice, and might disperse her doubts. . . . Under the escort of four attendants, Valeria set off to the monastery, while Fabio remained at home, and wandered about the garden till his wife's return, trying to comprehend what had happened to her, and a victim to constant fear and wrath, and the pain of undefined suspicions. . . . More than once he went up to the pavilion; but Muzzio had not returned, and the Malay gazed at Fabio like a statue, obsequiously bowing his head, with a well-dissembled—so at least it seemed to Fabio —smile on his bronzed face. Meanwhile, Valeria had in confession told everything to her priest, not so much with shame as with horror. The priest heard her attentively, gave her his blessing, absolved her from her involuntary sin, but to himself he thought: 'Sorcery, the arts of the devil . . . the matter can't be left so,' . . . and he returned with Valeria to her villa, as though with the aim of completely pacifying and reassuring her. At the sight of the priest

Fabio was thrown into some agitation; but the experienced old man had thought out beforehand how he must treat him. When he was left alone with Fabio, he did not of course betray the secrets of the confessional, but he advised him if possible to get rid of the guest they had invited to their house, as by his stories, his songs, and his whole behaviour he was troubling the imagination of Valeria. Moreover, in the old man's opinion, Muzzio had not, he remembered, been very firm in the faith in former days, and having spent so long a time in lands unenlightened by the truths of Christianity, he might well have brought thence the contagion of false doctrine, might even have become conversant with secret magic arts; and, therefore, though long friendship had indeed its claims, still a wise prudence pointed to the necessity of separation. Fabio fully agreed with the excellent monk. Valeria was even joyful when her husband reported to her the priest's counsel; and sent on his way with the cordial good-will of both the young people, loaded with good gifts for the monastery and the poor, Father Lorenzo returned home.

Fabio intended to have an explanation with Muzzio immediately after supper; but his strange guest did not return to supper. Then Fabio decided to defer his conversation with

Muzzio until the following day; and both the young people retired to rest

IX

VALERIA soon fell asleep; but Fabio could not sleep. In the stillness of the night, everything he had seen, everything he had felt presented itself more vividly; he put to himself still more insistently questions to which as before he could find no answer. Had Muzzio really become a sorcerer, and had he not already poisoned Valeria? She was ill . . . but what was her disease? While he lay, his head in his hand, holding his feverish breath, and given up to painful reflection, the moon rose again upon a cloudless sky; and together with its beams, through the half-transparent window-panes, there began, from the direction of the pavilion —or was it Fabio's fancy?—to come a breath, like a light, fragrant current . . . then an urgent, passionate murmur was heard . . . and at that instant he observed that Valeria was beginning faintly to stir. He started, looked; she rose up, slid first one foot, then the other out of the bed, and like one bewitched of the moon, her sight-less eyes fixed lifelessly before her, her hands

stretched out, she began moving towards the garden! Fabio instantly ran out of the other door
of the room, and running quickly round the corner
of the house, bolted the door that led into the
garden. . . . He had scarcely time to grasp at
the bolt, when he felt some one trying to open
the door from the inside, pressing against it . . .
again and again . . . and then there was the
sound of piteous passionate moans . . .

'But Muzzio has not come back from the
town,' flashed through Fabio's head, and he
rushed to the pavilion . . .

What did he see?

Coming towards him, along the path daz-
zlingly lighted up by the moon's rays, was
Muzzio, he too moving like one moonstruck, his
hands held out before him, and his eyes open but
unseeing. . . . Fabio ran up to him, but he, not
heeding him, moved on, treading evenly, step
by step, and his rigid face smiled in the moonlight like the Malay's. Fabio would have called
him by his name . . . but at that instant he
heard, behind him in the house, the creaking of
a window. . . . He looked round. . . .

Yes, the window of the bedroom was open
from top to bottom, and putting one foot over
the sill, Valeria stood in the window . . . her
hands seemed to be seeking Muzzio . . . she
seemed striving all over towards him. . . .

Unutterable fury filled Fabio's breast with a sudden inrush. 'Accursed sorcerer!' he shrieked furiously, and seizing Muzzio by the throat with one hand, with the other he felt for the dagger in his girdle, and plunged the blade into his side up to the hilt.

Muzzio uttered a shrill scream, and clapping his hand to the wound, ran staggering back to the pavilion. . . . But at the very same instant when Fabio stabbed him, Valeria screamed just as shrilly, and fell to the earth like grass before the scythe.

Fabio flew to her, raised her up, carried her to the bed, began to speak to her. . . .

She lay a long time motionless, but at last she opened her eyes, heaved a deep, broken, blissful sigh, like one just rescued from imminent death, saw her husband, and twining her arms about his neck, crept close to him. 'You, you, it is you,' she faltered. Gradually her hands loosened their hold, her head sank back, and murmuring with a blissful smile, 'Thank God, it is all over. . . . But how weary I am!' she fell into a sound but not heavy sleep.

X

FABIO sank down beside her bed, and never taking his eyes off her pale and sunken, but already calmer, face, began reflecting on what had happened . . . and also on how he ought to act now. What steps was he to take? If he had killed Muzzio—and remembering how deeply the dagger had gone in, he could have no doubt of it—it could not be hidden. He would have to bring it to the knowledge of the archduke, of the judges . . . but how explain, how describe such an incomprehensible affair? He, Fabio, had killed in his own house his own kinsman, his dearest friend? They will inquire, What for? on what ground? . . . But if Muzzio were not dead? Fabio could not endure to remain longer in uncertainty, and satisfying himself that Valeria was asleep, he cautiously got up from his chair, went out of the house, and made his way to the pavilion. Everything was still in it; only in one window a light was visible. With a sinking heart he opened the outer door (there was still the print of blood-stained fingers on it, and there were black drops of gore on the sand of the path), passed through the first dark room . . . and stood still on the threshold, overwhelmed with amazement.

In the middle of the room, on a Persian rug, with a brocaded cushion under his head, and all his limbs stretched out straight, lay Muzzio, covered with a wide, red shawl with a black pattern on it. His face, yellow as wax, with closed eyes and bluish eyelids, was turned towards the ceiling, no breathing could be discerned: he seemed a corpse. At his feet knelt the Malay, also wrapt in a red shawl. He was holding in his left hand a branch of some unknown plant, like a fern, and bending slightly forward, was gazing fixedly at his master. A small torch fixed on the floor burnt with a greenish flame, and was the only light in the room. The flame did not flicker nor smoke. The Malay did not stir at Fabio's entry, he merely turned his eyes upon him, and again bent them upon Muzzio. From time to time he raised and lowered the branch, and waved it in the air, and his dumb lips slowly parted and moved as though uttering soundless words. On the floor between the Malay and Muzzio lay the dagger, with which Fabio had stabbed his friend; the Malay struck one blow with the branch on the blood-stained blade. A minute passed . . . another. Fabio approached the Malay, and stooping down to him, asked in an undertone, 'Is he dead?' The Malay bent his head from above downwards, and disentangling his right hand from his shawl, he pointed imperiously to the door. Fabio would have repeated his question, but the gesture of the commanding hand was repeated, and Fabio went out, indignant and wondering, but obedient

He found Valeria sleeping as before, with an even more tranquil expression on her face. He did not undress, but seated himself by the window, his head in his hand, and once more sank into thought. The rising sun found him still in the same place. Valeria had not waked up.

XI

FABIO intended to wait till she awakened, and then to set off to Ferrara, when suddenly some one tapped lightly at the bedroom door. Fabio went out, and saw his old steward, Antonio. 'Signor,' began the old man, 'the Malay has just informed me that Signor Muzzio has been taken ill, and wishes to be moved with all his belongings to the town; and that he begs you to let him have servants to assist in packing his things; and that at dinner-time you would send pack-horses, and saddle-horses, and a few

attendants for the journey. Do you allow it?'
'The Malay informed you of this?' asked
Fabio. 'In what manner? Why, he is dumb.'
'Here, signor, is the paper on which he wrote
all this in our language, and very correctly.'
'And Muzzio, you say, is ill?' 'Yes, he is very
ill, and can see no one.' 'Have they sent for a
doctor?' 'No. The Malay forbade it.' 'And
was it the Malay wrote you this?' 'Yes, it
was he.' Fabio did not speak for a moment.
'Well, then, arrange it all,' he said at last.
Antonio withdrew.

Fabio looked after his servant in bewilderment. 'Then, he is not dead?' he thought
. . . and he did not know whether to rejoice or
to be sorry. 'Ill?' But a few hours ago it
was a corpse he had looked upon!

Fabio returned to Valeria. She waked up
and raised her head. The husband and wife
exchanged a long look full of significance.
'He is gone?' Valeria said suddenly. Fabio
shuddered. 'How gone? Do you mean . . .'
'Is he gone away?' she continued. A load fell
from Fabio's heart. 'Not yet; but he is going
to-day.' 'And I shall never, never see him
again?' 'Never.' 'And these dreams will
not come again?' 'No.' Valeria again heaved
a sigh of relief; a blissful smile once more
appeared on her lips. She held out both hands

to her husband. 'And we will never speak of him, never, do you hear, my dear one? And I will not leave my room till he is gone. And do you now send me my maids . . . but stay: take away that thing!' she pointed to the pearl necklace, lying on a little bedside table, the necklace given her by Muzzio, 'and throw it at once into our deepest well. Embrace me. I am your Valeria; and do not come in to me till . . . he has gone.' Fabio took the necklace —the pearls he fancied looked tarnished—and did as his wife had directed. Then he fell to wandering about the garden, looking from a distance at the pavilion, about which the bustle of preparations for departure was beginning. Servants were bringing out boxes, loading the horses . . . but the Malay was not among them. An irresistible impulse drew Fabio to look once more upon what was taking place in the pavilion. He recollected that there was at the back a secret door, by which he could reach the inner room where Muzzio had been lying in the morning. He stole round to this door found it unlocked, and, parting the folds of a heavy curtain, turned a faltering glance upon the room within.

XII

Muzzio was not now lying on the rug. Dressed as though for a journey, he sat in an arm-chair, but seemed a corpse, just as on Fabio's first visit. His torpid head fell back on the chair, and his outstretched hands hung lifeless, yellow, and rigid on his knees. His breast did not heave. Near the chair on the floor, which was strewn with dried herbs, stood some flat bowls of dark liquid, which exhaled a powerful, almost suffocating, odour, the odour of musk. Around each bowl was coiled a small snake of brazen hue, with golden eyes that flashed from time to time; while directly facing Muzzio, two paces from him, rose the long figure of the Malay, wrapt in a mantle of many-coloured brocade, girt round the waist with a tiger's tail, with a high hat of the shape of a pointed tiara on his head. But he was not motionless: at one moment he bowed down reverently, and seemed to be praying, at the next he drew himself up to his full height, even rose on tiptoe; then, with a rhythmic action, threw wide his arms, and moved them persistently in the direction of Muzzio, and seemed to threaten or command him, frowning and stamping with his foot. All these actions seemed to cost him great effort, even to cause him pain: he breathed heavily, the sweat streamed down his face. All at once he sank down to the ground, and drawing in a full breath, with knitted brow and immense effort, drew his clenched hands towards him, as though he were holding reins in them . . . and to the indescribable horror of Fabio, Muzzio's head slowly left the back of the chair, and moved forward, following the Malay's hands. . . . The Malay let them fall, and Muzzio's head fell heavily back again; the Malay repeated his movements, and obediently the head repeated them after him. The dark liquid in the bowls began boiling; the bowls themselves began to resound with a faint bell-like note, and the brazen snakes coiled freely about each of them. Then the Malay took a step forward, and raising his eyebrows and opening his eyes immensely wide, he bowed his head to Muzzio . . . and the eyelids of the dead man quivered, parted uncertainly, and under them could be seen the eyeballs, dull as lead. The Malay's face was radiant with triumphant pride and delight, a delight almost malignant; he opened his mouth wide, and from the depths of his chest there broke out with effort a prolonged howl. . . . Muzzio's lips parted too, and a faint moan quivered on them in response to that inhuman sound. . . .

But at this point Fabio could endure it no longer; he imagined he was present at some devilish incantation! He too uttered a shriek and rushed out, running home, home as quick as possible, without looking round, repeating prayers and crossing himself as he ran.

XIII

THREE hours later, Antonio came to him with the announcement that everything was ready, the things were packed, and Signor Muzzio was preparing to start Without a word in answer to his servant, Fabio went out on to the terrace, whence the pavilion could be seen. A few pack-horses were grouped before it; a powerful raven horse, saddled for two riders, was led up to the steps, where servants were standing bare-headed, together with armed attendants. The door of the pavilion opened, and supported by the Malay, who wore once more his ordinary attire, appeared Muzzio. His face was death-like, and his hands hung like a dead man's—but he walked . . . yes, positively walked, and, seated on the charger, he sat upright and felt for and found the reins The Malay put his feet in the stirrups, leaped up behind him on the saddle, put his arm round him, and the whole party started. The horses moved at a walking pace, and when they turned round before the house, Fabio fancied that in Muzzio's dark face there gleamed two spots of white. . . . Could it be he had turned his eyes upon him? Only the Malay bowed to him . . . ironically, as ever.

Did Valeria see all this? The blinds of her windows were drawn . . . but it may be she was standing behind them.

XIV

At dinner-time she came into the dining-room, and was very quiet and affectionate; she still complained, however, of weariness. But there was no agitation about her now, none of her former constant bewilderment and secret dread; and when, the day after Muzzio's departure, Fabio set to work again on her portrait, he found in her features the pure expression, the momentary eclipse of which had so troubled him . . . and his brush moved lightly and faithfully over the canvas.

The husband and wife took up their old life again. Muzzio vanished for them as though he had never existed. Fabio and Valeria were agreed, as it seemed, not to utter a syllable referring to him, not to learn anything of his later days; his fate remained, however, a mystery for alL Muzzio did actually disappear, as though he had sunk into the earth. Fabio one day thought it his duty to tell Valeria exactly what had taken place on that fatal night . . . but she probably divined his intention, and she held her breath, half-shutting her eyes, as though she were expecting a blow. . . . And Fabio understood her; he did not inflict that blow upon her.

One fine autumn day, Fabio was putting the last touches to his picture of his Cecilia; Valeria sat at the organ, her fingers straying at random over keys. . . . Suddenly, her knowing it, from under her hands came the first notes of that song of triumphant love which Muzzio had once played; and at the same instant, for the first time since her marriage, she felt within her the throb of a new palpitating life. . . . Valeria started, stopped. . . .

What did it mean? Could it be . . .

At this word the manuscript ended.

THE DREAM

THE DREAM

I WAS living at that time with my mother in a
little seaside town. I was in my seventeenth
year, while my mother was not quite five-and-
thirty; she had married very young. When
my father died, I was only seven years old, but
I remember him well. My mother was a fair-
haired woman, not very tall, with a charming,
but alway sad-looking face, a soft, tired voice
and timid gestures. In her youth she had been
reputed a beauty, and to the end she remained
attractive and pretty. I have never seen deeper,
tenderer, and sadder eyes, finer and softer hair;
I never saw hands so exquisite. I adored her,
and she loved me. . . . But our life was not
a bright one; a secret, hopeless, undeserved
sorrow seemed for ever gnawing at the very
root of her being. This sorrow could not be
accounted for by the loss of my father simply,
great as that loss was to her, passionately as my

mother had loved him, and devoutly as she had cherished his memory. . . . No! something more lay hidden in it, which I did not understand, but of which I was aware, dimly and yet intensely aware, whenever I looked into those soft and unchanging eyes, at those lips, unchanging too, not compressed in bitterness, but, as it were, for ever set in one expression.

I have said that my mother loved me; but there were moments when she repulsed me, when my presence was oppressive to her, unendurable. At such times she felt a sort of involuntary aversion for me, and was horrified afterwards, blamed herself with tears, pressed me to her heart. I used to ascribe these momentary outbreaks of dislike to the derangement of her health, to her unhappiness. . . . These antagonistic feelings might indeed, to some extent, have been evoked by certain strange outbursts of wicked and criminal passions, which arose from time to time in me, though I could not myself account for them. . . .

But these evil outbursts were never coincident with the moments of aversion. My mother always wore black, as though in mourning. We were in fairly good circumstances, but we hardly knew any one.

II

My mother concentrated her every thought, her every care, upon me. Her life was wrapped up in my life. That sort of relation between parents and children is not always good for the children . . . it is rather apt to be harmful to them. Besides, I was my mother's only son . . . and only children generally grow up in a one-sided way. In bringing them up, the parents think as much of themselves as of them. . . . That's not the right way. I was neither spoiled nor made hard by it (one or the other is apt to be the fate of only children), but my nerves were unhinged for a time; moreover, I was rather delicate in health, taking after my mother, whom I was very like in face. I avoided the companionship of boys of my own age; I held aloof from people altogether; even with my mother I talked very little. I liked best reading, solitary walks, and dreaming, dreaming! What my dreams were about, it would be hard to say; sometimes, indeed, I seemed to stand at a half-open door, beyond which lay unknown mysteries, to stand and wait, half dead with emotion, and not to step over the threshold, but still pondering what lay beyond, still to wait till I turned faint . . . or fell asleep. If there had been a vein of poetry in me, I should probably have taken to writing verses; if I had felt an inclination for religion, I should perhaps have gone into a monastery; but I had no tendency of the sort, and I went on dreaming and waiting.

III

I HAVE just mentioned that I used sometimes to fall asleep under the influence of vague dreams and reveries. I used to sleep a great deal at all times, and dreams played an important part in my life; I used to have dreams almost every night. I did not forget them, I attributed a significance to them, regarded them as fore-warnings, tried to divine their secret meaning; some of them were repeated from time to time, which always struck me as strange and marvellous. I was particularly perplexed by one dream. I dreamed I was going along a narrow, ill-paved street of an old-fashioned town, between stone houses of many stories, with pointed roofs. I was looking for my father, who was not dead, but, for some reason or other, hiding away from us, and living in one of these very houses. And so I entered a low, dark gateway, crossed a long courtyard, lumbered up with planks and beams, and made my way at last into a little room with two round windows. In the middle of the room stood my father in a dressing-gown, smoking a pipe. He was not in the least like my real father; he was tall and thin, with black hair, a hook nose, with sullen and piercing eyes; he looked about forty. He was displeased at my having found him; and I too was far from being delighted at our meeting, and stood still in perplexity. He turned a little away, began muttering something, and walking up and down with short steps . . . Then he gradually got farther away, never ceasing his muttering, and continually looking back over his shoulder; the room grew larger and was lost in fog. . . . I felt all at once horrified at the idea that I was losing my father again, and rushed after him, but I could no longer see him, I could only hear his angry muttering, like a bear growling. . . . My heart sank with dread; I woke up and could not for a long while get to sleep again. . . . All the following day I pondered on this dream, and naturally could make nothing of it.

IV

THE month of June had come. The town in which I was living with my mother became exceptionally lively about that time. A number of ships were in the harbour, a number of new faces were to be seen in the streets. I liked at such times to wander along the sea front, by cafés and hotels, to stare at the widely differing figures of the sailors and other people, sitting under linen awnings, at small white tables, with pewter pots of beer before them.

As I passed one day before a café, I caught sight of a man who at once riveted my whole attention. Dressed in a long black full coat, with a straw hat pulled right down over his eyes, he was sitting perfectly still, his arms folded across his chest The straggling curls of his black hair fell almost down to his nose; his thin lips held tight the mouthpiece of a short pipe. This man struck me as so familiar, every feature of his swarthy yellow face were so unmistakably imprinted in my memory, that I could not help stopping short before him, I could not help asking myself, 'Who is that man? where have I seen him?' Becoming aware, probably, of my intent stare, he raised his black, piercing eyes upon me. . . . I uttered an involuntary 'Ah!' . . .

The man was the father I had been looking for, the father I had beheld in my dream!

There was no possibility of mistake—the resemblance was too striking. The very coat even, that wrapped his spare limbs in its long skirts, in hue and cut, recalled the dressing-gown in which my father had appeared in the dream.

'Am I not asleep now?' I wondered. . . . No. . . . It was daytime, about me crowds of people were bustling, the sun was shining brightly in the blue sky, and before me was no phantom, but a living man.

I went up to an empty table, asked for a pot of beer and a newspaper, and sat down not far off from this enigmatical being.

V

PUTTING the sheet of newspaper on a level with my face, I continued my scrutiny of the stranger. He scarcely stirred at all, only from time to time raising his bowed head. He was obviously expecting some one. I gazed and gazed. . . . Sometimes I fancied I must have imagined it all, that there could be really no resemblance, that I had given way to a half-unconscious trick of the imagination . . . but the stranger would suddenly turn round a little in his seat, or slightly raise his hand, and again I all but cried out, again I saw my 'dream-father' before me! He at last noticed my uncalled-for attention, and glancing at first with surprise and then with annoyance in my direction, was on the point of getting up, and knocked down a small walking-stick he had stood against the table. I instantly jumped up, picked it up, and handed it to him. My heart was beating violently.

He gave a constrained smile, thanked me, and as his face drew closer to my face, he lifted his eyebrows and opened his mouth a little as though struck by something.

'You are very polite, young man,' he began all at once in a dry, incisive, nasal voice. 'That's something out of the common nowadays. Let me congratulate you; you must have been well brought up?'

I don't remember precisely what answer I made; but a conversation soon sprang up between us. I learnt that he was a fellow-countryman, that he had not long returned from America, where he had spent many years, and was shortly going back there. He called himself Baron . . . the name I could not make out distinctly. He, just like my 'dream-father,' ended every remark with a sort of indistinct inward mutter. He desired to learn my sur-name. . . . On hearing it, he seemed again astonished; then he asked me if I had lived long in the town, and with whom I was living. I told him I was living with my mother.

'And your father?' 'My father died long ago.' He inquired my mother's Christian name, and immediately gave an awkward laugh, but apologised, saying that he picked up some American ways, and was rather a queer fellow altogether. Then he was curious to know what was our address. I told him.

VI

THE excitement which had possessed me at the beginning of our conversation gradually calmed down; I felt our meeting rather strange and nothing more. I did not like the little smile with which the baron cross-examined me; I did not like the expression of his eyes when he, as it were, stuck them like pins into me. . . . There was something in them rapacious, patronising . . . something unnerving. Those eyes I had not seen in the dream. A strange face was the baron's! Faded, fatigued, and, at the same time, young-looking—unpleasantly young-looking! My 'dream-father' had not the deep scar either which ran slanting right across my new acquaintance's forehead, and which I had not noticed till I came closer to him.

I had hardly told the baron the name of the street, and the number of the house in which we were living, when a tall negro, swathed up to the eyebrows in a cloak, came up to him from behind, and softly tapped him on the shoulder. The baron turned round, ejaculated, 'Aha! at last!' and with a slight nod to me, went with the negro into the café. I was left under the awning; I meant to await the baron's return, not so much with the object of entering into conversation with him again (I really did not know what to talk about to him), as to verify once more my first impression. But half-an-hour passed, an hour passed. . . . The baron did not appear. I went into the café, passed through all the rooms, but could see nowhere the baron or the negro. . . . They must both have gone out by a back-door.

My head ached a little, and to get a little fresh air, I walked along the seafront to a large park outside the town, which had been laid out two hundred years ago.

After strolling for a couple of hours in the shade of the immense oaks and plane-trees, I returned home.

VII

Our maid-servant rushed all excitement, to meet me, directly I appeared in the hall; I guessed at once from the expression of her face, that during my absence something had gone wrong in our house. And, in fact, I learnt that an hour before, a fearful shriek had suddenly been heard in my mother's bedroom, the maid running in had found her on the floor in a fainting fit, which had lasted several moments. My mother had at last regained consciousness, but had been obliged to lie down, and looked strange and scared; she had not uttered a word, had not answered inquiries, she had done nothing but look about her and shudder. The maid had sent the gardener for a doctor. The doctor came and prescribed soothing treatment; but my mother would say nothing even to him. The gardener maintained that, a few instants after the shriek was heard in my mother's room, he had seen a man, unknown to him, running through the bushes in the garden to the gate into the street. (We lived in a house of one story, with windows opening on to a rather large garden.) The gardener had not time to get a look at the man's face; but he was tall, and was wearing a low straw hat and long coat with full skirts . . . 'The baron's costume!' at once crossed my mind. The gardener could not overtake him; besides, he had been immediately called into the house and sent for the doctor. I went in to my mother; she was lying on the bed, whiter than the pillow on which her head was resting. Recognising me, she smiled faintly, and held out her hand to me. I sat down beside her, and began to question her; at first she said no to everything; at last she admitted, however, that she had seen something which had greatly terrified her. 'Did some one come in here?' I asked. 'No,' she hurriedly replied—'no one came in, it was my fancy . . . an apparition . . .' She ceased and hid her face in her hands. I was on the paint of telling her, what I had learnt from the gardener, and incidentally describing my meeting with the baron . . . but for some reason or other, the words died away on my lips, I ventured, however, to observe to my mother, that apparitions do not usually appear in the daytime. . . . 'Stop,' she whispered, 'please; do not torture me now. You will know some time . . . .' She was silent again. Her hands were cold and her pulse beat fast and unevenly. I gave her some medicine and moved a little away so as not to disturb her. She did not get up the whole day. She lay perfectly still and quiet, and now and then heaving a deep sigh, and timorously opening her eyes. Everyone in the house was at a loss what to think.

VIII

TOWARDS night my mother became a little feverish, and she sent me away. I did not, however, go to my own room, but lay down in the next room on the sofa. Every quarter of an hour I got up, went on tiptoe to the door, listened. . . . Everything was still—but my mother hardly slept that night. When I went in to her early in the morning, her face looked hollow, her eyes shone with an unnatural brightness. In the course of the day she got a little better, but towards evening the feverishness increased again. Up till then she had been obstinately silent, but all of a sudden she began talking in a hurried broken voice. She was not wandering, there was a meaning in her words—but no sort of connection. Just upon midnight, she suddenly, with a convulsive movement raised herself in bed—I was sitting beside her—and in the same hurried voice, continually taking sips of water, from a glass beside her, feebly gesticulating with her hands, and never once looking at me, she began to tell her story. . . . She would stop, make an effort to control herself and go on again. . . . It was all so strange, just as though she were doing it all in a dream, as though she herself were absent, and some one else were speaking by her lips, or forcing her to speak.

IX

'LISTEN to what I am going to tell you,' she began. 'You are not a little boy now; you ought to know all. I had a friend, a girl . . . She married a man she loved with all her heart, and she was very happy with her husband. During the first year of their married life they went together to the capital to spend a few weeks there and enjoy themselves. They stayed at a good hotel, and went out a great deal to theatres and parties. My friend was very pretty—every one noticed her, young men paid her attentions,—but there was among them one . . . an officer. He followed her about incessantly, and wherever she was, she always saw his cruel black eyes. He was not introduced to her, and never once spoke to her —only perpetually stared at her—so insolently and strangely. All the pleasures of the capital were poisoned by his presence. She began persuading her husband to hasten their departure— and they had already made all the preparations for the journey. One evening her husband went out to a club—he had been invited by the officers of the same regiment as that officer—to play cards. . . . She was for the very first time left alone. Her husband did not return for a long while. She dismissed her maid, and went to bed. . . . And suddenly she felt overcome by terror, so that she was quite cold and shivering. She fancied she heard a slight sound on the other side of the wall, like a dog scratching, and she began watching the wall. In the corner a lamp was burning; the room was all hung with tapestry. . . . Suddenly something stirred there, rose, opened. . . . And straight out of the wall a black, long figure came, that awful man with the cruel eyes! She tried to scream, but could not. She was utterly numb with terror. He went up to her

rapidly, like some beast of prey, flung something
on her head, something strong-smelling, heavy,
white . . . What happened then I don't remember . . . I don't remember! It was like
death, like a murder . . . When at last that
fearful darkness began to pass away—when I
. . . when my friend came to herself, there was
no one in the room. Again, and for a long
time, she had not the strength to scream, she
screamed at last . . . then again everything
was confusion. . . . Then she saw her husband
by her side: he had been kept at the club till
two o'clock at night . . . He looked scared and
white. He began questioning her, but she told
him nothing. . . . Then she swooned away
again. I remember though when she was left
alone in the room, she examined the place in
the wall. . . . Under the tapestry hangings it
turned out there was a secret door. And her
betrothal ring had gone from off her hand.
This ring was of an unusual pattern; seven
little gold stars alternated on it with seven silver
stars; it was an old family heirloom. Her
husband asked her what had become of the
ring; she could give him no answer. Her
husband supposed she had dropped it somewhere, searched everywhere, but could not find
it He felt uneasy and distressed; he decided
to go home as soon as possible and directly

the doctor allowed it—they left the capital. . . .
But imagine! On the very day of their
departure they happened suddenly to meet a
stretcher being carried along the street. . . . On
the stretcher lay a man who had just been
killed, with his head cut open; and imagine!
the man was that fearful apparition of the
night with the evil eyes. . . . He had been
killed over some gambling dispute!

Then my friend went away into the country
. . . became a mother for the first time . . .
and lived several years with her husband. He
never knew anything; indeed, what could she
have told him?—she knew nothing herself.

But her former happiness had vanished. A
gloom had come over their lives, and never
again did that gloom pass out of it. . . . They
had no other children, either before or after
. . . and that son . . .'

My mother trembled all over and hid her face
in her hands.

'But say now,' she went on with redoubled
energy, 'was my friend to blame in any way?
What had she to reproach herself with? She
was punished, but had she not the right to
declare before God Himself that the punish-
ment that overtook her was unjust? Then why
is it, that like a criminal, tortured by stings of
conscience, why is it she is confronted with the

past in such a fearful shape after so many years? Macbeth slew Bancho—so no wonder that he could be haunted . . . but I . . .'

But here my mother's words became so mixed and confused, that I ceased to follow her. . . . I no longer doubted that she was in delirium.

X

THE agitating effect of my mother's recital on me—any one may easily conceive! I guessed from her first word that she was talking of herself, and not any friend of hers. Her slip of the tongue confirmed my conjecture. Then this really was my father, whom I was seeking in my dream, whom I had seen awake by daylight! He had not been killed, as my mother supposed, but only wounded. And he had come to see her, and had run away, alarmed by her alarm. I suddenly understood everything: the feeling of involuntary aversion for me, which arose at times in my mother, and her perpetual melancholy, and our secluded life. . . . I remember my head seemed going round, and I clutched it in both hands as though to hold it still. But one idea, as it were, nailed me down; I resolved I must, come what may, find that

218

man again? What for? with what aim? I
could not give myself a clear answer, but to
find him . . . find him—that had become a
question of life and death for me! The next
morning my mother, at last, grew calmer . . .
the fever left her . . . she fell asleep. Confid-
ing her to the care of the servants and people
of the house, I set out on my quest

XI

FIRST of all I made my way, of course, to the
café where I had met the baron; but no one in
the café knew him or had even noticed him; he
had been a chance customer there. The negro
the people there had observed, his figure was so
striking; but who he was, and where he was
staying, no one knew. Leaving my address
in any case at the café, I fell to wandering
about the streets and sea front by the harbour,
along the boulevards, peeped into all places of
public resort, but could find no one like the
baron or his companion! . . . Not having
caught the baron's surname, I was deprived of
the resource of applying to the police; I did,
however, privately let two or three guardians of
the public safety know—they stared at me in

bewilderment, and did not altogether believe in
me—that I would reward them liberally if they
could trace out two persons, whose exterior I
tried to describe as exactly as possible. After
wandering about in this way till dinner-time,
I returned home exhausted. My mother had
got up; but to her usual melancholy there was
added something new, a sort of dreamy blank-
ness, which cut me to the heart like a knife. I
spent the evening with her. We scarcely spoke
at all; she played patience, I looked at her
cards in silence. She never made a single
reference to what she had told me, nor to what
had happened the preceding evening. It was
as though we had made a secret compact not
to touch on any of these harrowing and strange
incidents. . . . She seemed angry with herself,
and ashamed of what had broken from her
unawares; though possibly she did not remember quite what she had said in her half delirious feverishness, and hoped I should spare her.
. . . And indeed this was it, I spared her, and
she felt it; as on the previous day she avoided
my eyes. I could not get to sleep all night.
Outside, a fearful storm suddenly came on.
The wind howled and darted furiously hither
and thither, the window-panes rattled and rang,
despairing shrieks and groans sounded in the
air, as though something had been torn to

shreds up aloft, and were flying with frenzied
wailing over the shaken houses. Before dawn
I dropped off into a doze . . . suddenly I
fancied some one came into my room, and
called me, uttered my name, in a voice not
loud, but resolute. I raised my head and saw
no one; but, strange to say! I was not only
not afraid—I was glad; I suddenly felt a conviction that now I should certainly attain my
object I dressed hurriedly and went out of the
house.

XII

THE storm had abated . . . but its last struggles
could still be felt It was very early, there
were no people in the streets, many places were
strewn with broken chimney-pots and tiles,
pieces of wrecked fencing, and branches of
trees. . . . 'What was it like last night at sea?'
I could not help wondering at the sight of the
traces left by the storm. I intended to go to
the harbour, but my legs, as though in obedience
to some irresistible attraction, carried me in
another direction. Ten minutes had not gone
by before I found myself in a part of the town
I had never visited till then. I walked not

rapidly, but without halting, step by step, with a strange sensation at my heart; I expected something extraordinary, impossible, and at the same time I was convinced that this extraordinary thing would come to pass.

XIII

AND, behold, it came to pass, this extraordinary, this unexpected thing! Suddenly, twenty paces before me, I saw the very negro who had addressed the baron in the café! Muffled in the same cloak as I had noticed on him there, he seemed to spring out of the earth, and with his back turned to me, walked with rapid strides along the narrow pavement of the winding street. I promptly flew to overtake him, but he, too, redoubled his pace, though he did not look round, and all of a sudden turned sharply round the corner of a projecting house. I ran up to this corner, turned round it as quickly as the negro . . . Wonderful to relate! I faced a long, narrow, perfectly empty street; the fog of early morning filled it with its leaden dulness, but my eye reached to its very end, I could scan all the buildings in it . . . and not a living creature stirring anywhere! The tall negro in the cloak had vanished as suddenly as he had appeared! I was bewildered . . . but only for one instant. Another feeling at once took possession of me; the street, which stretched its length, dumb, and, as it were, dead, before my eyes, I knew it! It was the street of my dream. I started, shivered, the morning was so fresh, and promptly, without the least hesitation, with a sort of shudder of conviction, went on!

I began looking about. . . . Yes, here it was; here to the right, standing cornerwise to the street, was the house of my dream, here too the old-fashioned gateway with scrollwork in stone on both sides. . . . It is true the windows of the house were not round, but rectangular. . . . but that was not important . . . I knocked at the gate, knocked twice or three times, louder and louder. . . . The gate was opened slowly with a heavy groan as though yawning. I was confronted by a young servant girl with dishevelled hair, and sleepy eyes. She was apparently only just awake. 'Does the baron live here?' I asked, and took in with a rapid glance the deep narrow courtyard. . . . Yes; it was all there . . . there were the planks and beams I had seen in my dream.

'No,' the servant girl answered, 'the baron's not living here.'

'Not? impossible!'

'He's not here now. He left yesterday.'

'Where's he gone?'

'To America.'

'To America!' I repeated involuntarily. 'But he will come back?'

The servant looked at me suspiciously.

'We don't know about that. May be he won't come back at all.'

'And has he been living here long?'

'Not long, a week. He's not here now.'

'And what was his surname, the baron's?' The girl stared at me.

'You don't know his name? We simply called him the baron.—Hi! Piotr!' she shouted, seeing I was pushing in. 'Come here; here's a stranger keeps asking questions.'

From the house came the clumsy figure of a sturdy workman.

'What is it? What do you want?' he asked in a sleepy voice; and having heard me sullenly, he repeated what the girl had told me.

'But who does live here?' I asked.

'Our master.'

'Who is he?'

'A carpenter. They're all carpenters in this street.'

'Can I see him?'

'You can't now, he's asleep.'

'But can't I go into the house?'

'No. Go away.'

'Well, but can I see your master later on?'

'What for? Of course. You can always see him. . . . To be sure, he's always at his business here. Only go away now. Such a time in the morning, upon my soul!'

'Well, but that negro?' I asked suddenly.

The workman looked in perplexity first at me, then at the servant girl.

'What negro?' he said at last. 'Go away, sir. You can come later. You can talk to the master.'

I went out into the street. The gate slammed at once behind me, sharply and heavily, with no groan this time.

I carefully noted the street and the house, and went away, but not home—I was conscious of a sort of disillusionment. Everything that had happened to me was so strange, so unexpected, and meanwhile what a stupid conclusion to it! I had been persuaded, I had been convinced, that I should see in that house the room I knew, and in the middle of it my father, the baron, in the dressing-gown, and with a pipe. . . . And instead of that, the master of the house was a carpenter, and I could go and see him as much as I liked—and order furniture of him, I dare say.

225

My father had gone to America. And what was left for me to do? . . . To tell my mother everything, or to bury for ever the very memory of that meeting? I positively could not resign myself to the idea that such a supernatural, mysterious beginning should end in such a senseless, ordinary conclusion!

I did not want to return home, and walked at random away from the town.

XIV

I WALKED with downcast head, without thought, almost without sensation, but utterly buried in myself. A rhythmic hollow and angry noise raised me from my numbness. I lifted my head; it was the sea roaring and moaning fifty paces from me. I saw I was walking along the sand of the dunes. The sea, set in violent commotion by the storm in the night, was white with foam to the very horizon, and the sharp crests of the long billows rolled one after another and broke on the flat shore. I went nearer to it, and walked along the line left by the ebb and flow of the tides on the yellow furrowed sand, strewn with fragments of trailing seaweed, broken shells, and snakelike ribbons of sea-grass. Gulls, with pointed wings, flying with a plaintive cry on the wind out of the remote depths of the air, soared up, white as snow against the grey cloudy sky, fell abruptly, and seeming to leap from wave to wave, vanished again, and were lost like gleams of silver in the streaks of frothing foam. Several of them, I noticed, hovered persistently over a big rock, which stood up alone in the midst of the level uniformity of the sandy shore. Coarse seaweed was growing in irregular masses on one side of the rock; and where its matted tangles rose above the yellow line, was something black, something longish, curved, not very large. . . . I looked attentively. . . . Some dark object was lying there, lying motionless beside the rock. . . . This object grew clearer, more defined the nearer I got to it . . . .

There was only a distance of thirty paces left between me and the rock. . . . Why, it was the outline of a human form! It was a corpse; it was a drowned man thrown up by the sea! I went right up to the rock.

The corpse was the baron, my father! I stood as though turned to stone. Only then I realised that I had been led since early morning by some unknown forces, that I was in their power, and for some instants there was nothing in my soul but the never-ceasing crash of the sea, and dumb horror at the fate that had possession of me. . . .

XV

HE lay on his back, turned a little to one side, with his left arm behind his head . . . the right was thrust under his bent body. The toes of his feet, in high sailor's boots, had been sucked into the slimy sea-mud; the short blue jacket, drenched through with brine, was still closely buttoned; a red scarf was fastened in a tight knot about his neck. The dark face, turned to the sky, looked as if it were laughing, the small close-set teeth could be seen under the lifted upper lip; the dim pupils of the half-closed eyes were scarcely discernible in the darkened eyeballs; the clotted hair, covered with bubbles of foam, lay dishevelled on the ground, and bared the smooth brow with the purple line of the scar; the narrow nose rose, a sharp white line, between the sunken cheeks. The storm of the previous night had done its work. . . . He would never see America again! The man who had outraged my mother, who had spoiled and soiled her life; my father—yes!

my father—of that I could feel no doubt—lay helplessly outstretched in the mud at my feet. I experienced a sensation of satisfied revenge, and of pity, and repulsion, and horror, more than all . . . a double horror, at what I saw, and at what had happened. The wicked criminal feelings of which I have spoken, those uncomprehended impulses of rage rose up in me . . . choked me. 'Aha!' I thought, 'so that is why I am like this . . . that is how my blood shows itself!' I stood beside the corpse, and stared in suspense. Would not those dead eyes move, would not those stiff lips quiver? No! all was still; the very seaweed seemed lifeless where the breakers had flung it; even the gulls had flown; not a broken spar anywhere, not a fragment of wood, nor a bit of rigging. On all sides emptiness . . . only he and I, and in the distance the sounding sea. I looked back; the same emptiness there: a ridge of lifeless downs on the horizon . . . that was all! My heart revolted against leaving this luckless wretch in this solitude, on the briny sand of the seashore, to be devoured by fishes and birds; an inner voice told me I ought to find people, call them, if not to help—what help could there be now!—at least to lift him up, to carry him into some living habitation . . . but an indescribable panic suddenly seized on me. It

seemed to me that this dead man knew I had
come here, that he had himself planned this last
meeting. I even fancied I heard the indistinct
mutter I knew so well. . . . I ran away . . .
looked back once. . . . Something glittering
caught my eye; it brought me to a halt. It
was a hoop of gold on the hand of the corpse.
. . . I knew it for my mother's betrothal ring.
I remember how I forced myself to turn back,
to go up, to bend down . . . I remember the
clammy touch of the chill fingers; I remember
how I held my breath, and half-closed my
eyes, and set my teeth, tearing off the obstinate
ring . . .

At last, it was off . . . and I was running,
running away at full speed, with something
flying behind me, upon my heels, overtaking
me.

XVI

ALL I had felt and gone through was probably
written on my face when I got home. My
mother abruptly drew herself up directly I went
into her room, and looked with such urgent
inquiry at me, that, after an unsuccessful
attempt to explain, I ended by holding out
the ring to her in silence. She turned fear-

fully white, her eyes opened extraordinarily and looked dead, like *those* eyes; she uttered a faint cry, snatched the ring; reeled, fell on my breast, and fairly swooned away, her head falling back, and her blank wide-open eyes staring at me. I threw both my arms about her, and standing where I was, without moving, told her slowly, in a subdued voice, everything, without the slightest concealment: my dream, and the meeting, and everything, everything. . . . She heard me to the end without uttering a single word, only her bosom heaved more and more violently, and her eyes suddenly flashed and sank. Then she put the ring on her third finger, and, moving away a little, began getting her cape and hat. I asked her where she was going. She lifted eyes full of surprise upon me, and tried to answer, but her voice failed her. She shuddered several times, rubbed her hands, as though she were trying to warm them, and at last said, 'Let us go there at once.'

'Where, mother?'

'Where he is lying . . . I want to see . . . I want to know . . . I will know . . .'

I endeavoured to persuade her not to go; but she almost fell into a nervous attack. I saw it was impossible to oppose her wish, and we set off.

XVII

AND now I was again walking along the sand; but this time not alone. I had my mother on my arm. The sea had ebbed away, had retreated farther still; it was calmer, but its roar, though fainter, was still menacing and malignant. There, at last, rose the solitary rock before us; there was the seaweed too. I looked intently, I tried to distinguish that curved object lying on the ground—but I saw nothing. We went closer; instinctively I slackened my pace. But where was the black still object? Only the tangles of seaweed rose black against the sand, which had dried up by now. We went right up to the rock. . . . There was no corpse to be seen; and only where it had been lying there was still a hollow place, and one could see where the arms and where the legs had lain. . . . The seaweed around looked as it were crushed, and prints were visible of one man's feet; they crossed the dune, then were lost, as they reached the heaped-up shingle.

My mother and I looked at each other, and were frightened at what we saw in each other's faces. . . .

Surely he had not got up of himself and gone away?

'You are sure you saw him dead?' she asked in a whisper.

I could only nod in assent. hours had not passed since I had come upon the baron's corpse. . . . Some one had discovered and removed it. I must find out who had done it, and what had become of it.

But first I had to look after my mother.

XVIII

WHILE she had been walking to the fatal spot she had been in a fever, but she controlled herself. The disappearance of the dead body came upon her as a final blow. She was struck dumb. I feared for her reason. With great difficulty I got her home. I made her lie down again on her bed, again I sent for the doctor, but as soon as my mother had recovered herself a little, she at one desired me to set off without delay to find out 'that man.' I obeyed. But, in spite of every possible effort, I discovered nothing. I went several times to the police, visited several villages in the neighbourhood, put several advertisements in the papers, col-

233

lected information in all directions, and all in
vain! I received information, indeed, that the
corpse of a drowned man had been picked up
in one of the seaside villages near. . . . I at
once hastened off there, but from all I could
hear the body had no resemblance to the baron.
I found out in what ship he had set sail for
America; at first every one was positive that
ship had gone down in the storm; but a few
months later there were rumours that it had
been seen riding at anchor in New York harbour. Not knowing what steps to take, I
began seeking out the negro I had seen, offering him in the papers a considerable sum of
money if he would call at our house. Some
tall negro in a cloak did actually call on us in
my absence. . . . But after questioning the
maid, he abruptly departed, and never came
back again.

So all traces were lost of my . . . my father;
so he vanished into silence and darkness never
to return. My mother and I never spoke of
him; only one day, I remember, she expressed
surprise that I had never told her before of my
strange dream; and added, 'It must mean he
really . . .' but did not utter all her thought
My mother was ill a long while, and even after
her recovery our former close relations never
returned. She was ill at ease with me to the

day of her death. . . . Ill at ease was just what she was. And that is a trouble there is no cure for. Anything may be smoothed over, memories of even the most tragic domestic incidents gradually lose their strength and bitterness; but if once a sense of being ill at ease installs itself between two closely united persons, it can never be dislodged! I never again had the dream that had once so agitated me; I no longer 'look for' my father; but sometimes I fancied—and even now I fancy—that I hear, as it were, distant wails, as it were, never silent, mournful plaints; they seem to sound somewhere behind a high wall, which cannot be crossed; they wring my heart, and I weep with closed eyes, and am never able to tell what it is, whether it is a living man moaning, or whether I am listening to the wild, long-drawn-out howl of the troubled sea. And then it passes again into the muttering of some beast, and I fall asleep with anguish and horror in my heart.

1876.

POEMS IN PROSE

POEMS IN PROSE

I

[1878]

THE COUNTRY

THE last day of July; for a thousand versts around, Russia, our native land.

An unbroken blue flooding the whole sky; a single cloudlet upon it, half floating, half fading away. Windlessness, warmth . . . air like new milk!

Larks are trilling; pouter-pigeons cooing; noiselessly the swallows dart to and fro; horses are neighing and munching; the dogs do not bark and stand peaceably wagging their tails.

A smell of smoke and of hay, and a little of tar, too, and a little of hides. The hemp, now in full bloom, sheds its heavy, pleasant fragrance.

A deep but sloping ravine. Along its sides willows in rows, with big heads above, trunks cleft below. Through the ravine runs a brook; the tiny pebbles at its bottom are all aquiver through its clear eddies. In the distance, on the border-line between earth and heaven, the bluish streak of a great river.

Along the ravine, on one side, tidy barns, little storehouses with close-shut doors; on the other side, five or six pinewood huts with boarded roofs. Above each roof, the high pole of a pigeon-house; over each entry a little short-maned horse of wrought iron. The window-panes of faulty glass shine with all the colours of the rainbow. Jugs of flowers are painted on the shutters. Before each door, a little bench stands prim and neat; on the mounds of earth, cats are basking, their transparent ears pricked up alert; beyond the high door-sills, is the cool dark of the outer rooms.

I lie on the very edge of the ravine, on an outspread horse-cloth; all about are whole stacks of fresh-cut hay, oppressively fragrant. The sagacious husbandmen have flung the hay about before the huts; let it get a bit drier in the baking sunshine; and then into the barn with it. It will be first-rate sleeping on it.

Curly, childish heads are sticking out of every haycock; crested hens are looking in the hay for flies and little beetles, and a white-lipped pup is rolling among the tangled stalks.

Flaxen-headed lads in clean smocks, belted low, in heavy boots, leaning over an unharnessed waggon, fling each other smart volleys of banter, with broad grins showing their white teeth.

A round-faced young woman peeps out of window; laughs at their words or at the romps of the children in the mounds of hay.

Another young woman with powerful arms draws a great wet bucket out of the well. . . . The bucket quivers and shakes, spilling long, glistening drops.

Before me stands an old woman in a new striped petticoat and new shoes.

Fat hollow beads are wound in three rows about her dark thin neck, her grey head is tied up in a yellow kerchief with red spots; it hangs low over her failing eyes.

But there is a smile of welcome in the aged eyes; a smile all over the wrinkled face. The old woman has reached, I dare say, her seventieth year . . . and even now one can see she has been a beauty in her day.

With a twirl of her sunburnt finger, she holds in her right hand a bowl of cold milk, with the cream on it, fresh from the cellar; the sides of the bowl are covered with drops, like strings of pearls. In the palm of her left hand the old woman brings me a huge hunch of warm bread, as though to say, 'Eat, and welcome, passing guest!'

A cock suddenly crows and fussily flaps his wings; he is slowly answered by the low of a calf, shut up in the stall.

'My word, what oats!' I hear my coachman saying. . . . Oh, the content, the quiet, the plenty of the Russian open country! Oh, the deep peace and well-being!

And the thought comes to me: what is it all to us here, the cross on the cupola of St. Sophia in Constantinople and all the rest that we are struggling for, we men of the town?

A CONVERSATION

'Neither the Jungfrau nor the Finsteraarhorn has yet been trodden by the foot of man!'

THE topmost peaks of the Alps. . . . A whole chain of rugged precipices. . . . The very heart of the mountains.

Over the mountain, a pale green, clear, dumb sky. Bitter, cruel frost; hard, sparkling snow; sticking out of the snow, the sullen peaks of the ice-covered, wind-swept mountains.

Two massive forms, two giants on the sides

of the horizon, the Jungfrau and the Finsteraarhorn.

And the Jungfrau speaks to its neighbour:
'What canst thou tell that is new? thou canst
see more. What is there down below?'

A few thousand years go by: one minute.
And the Finsteraarhorn roars back in answer:
'Thick clouds cover the earth. . . . Wait a
little!'

Thousands more years go by: one minute.

'Well, and now?' asks the Jungfrau.

'Now I see, there below all is the same.
There are blue waters, black forests, grey heaps
of piled-up stones. Among them are still
fussing to and fro the insects, thou knowest,
the bipeds that have never yet once defiled
thee nor me.'

'Men?'

'Yes, men.'

Thousands of years go by: one minute.

'Well, and now?' asks the Jungfrau.

'There seem fewer insects to be seen,' thunders
the Finsteraarhorn, 'it is clearer down below;
the waters have shrunk, the forests are thinner.'
Again thousands of years go by: one minute.

'What seeest thou?' says the Jungfrau.

'Close about us it seems purer,' answers the
Finsteraarhorn, 'but there in the distance in the
valleys are still spots, and something is moving.'

'And now?' asks the Jungfrau, after more thousands of years: one minute.

'Now it is well,' answers the Finsteraarhorn, 'it is clean everywhere, quite white, wherever you look. . . . Everywhere is our snow, unbroken snow and ice. Everything is frozen. It is well now, it is quiet.'

'Good,' said the Jungfrau. 'But we have gossipped enough, old fellow. It's time to slumber.'

'It is time, indeed.'

The huge mountains sleep; the green, clear sky sleeps over the region of eternal silence.

February 1878.

THE OLD WOMAN

I was walking over a wide plain alone.

And suddenly I fancied light, cautious footsteps behind my back. . . . Some one was walking after me.

I looked round, and saw a little, bent old woman, all muffled up in grey rags. The face of the old woman alone peeped out from them; a yellow, wrinkled, sharp-nosed, toothless face.

I went up to her. . . . She stopped.

'Who are you? What do you want? Are you a beggar? Do you seek alms?'

The old woman did not answer. I bent down to her, and noticed that both her eyes were covered with a half-transparent membrane or skin, such as is seen in some birds; they protect their eyes with it from dazzling light.

But in the old woman, the membrane did not move nor uncover the eyes . . . from which I concluded she was blind.

'Do you want alms?' I repeated my question. 'Why are you following me?' But the old woman as before made no answer, but only shrank into herself a little.

I turned from her and went on my way.

And again I hear behind me the same light, measured, as it were, stealthy steps.

'Again that woman!' I thought, 'why does she stick to me?' But then, I added inwardly, 'Most likely she has lost her way, being blind, and now is following the sound of my steps so as to get with me to some inhabited place. Yes, yes, that's it.'

But a strange uneasiness gradually gained possession of my mind. I began to fancy that the old woman was not only following me, but that she was directing me, that she was driving me to right and to left, and that I was unwittingly obeying her.

I still go on, however . . . but, behold, before me, on my very road, something black and wide . . . a kind of hole. . . . 'A grave!' flashed through my head. 'That is where she is driving me!'

I turned sharply back. The old woman faced me again . . . but she sees! She is looking at me with big, cruel, malignant eyes . . . the eyes of a bird of prey. . . . I stoop down to her face, to her eyes. . . . Again the same opaque membrane, the same blind, dull countenance. . . .

'Ah!' I think, 'this old woman is my fate. The fate from which there is no escape for man!'

'No escape! no escape! What madness. . . . One must try.' And I rush away in another direction.

I go swiftly. . . . But light footsteps as before patter behind me, close, close. . . . And before me again the dark hole.

Again I turn another way. . . . And again the same patter behind, and the same menacing blur of darkness before.

And whichever way I run, doubling like a hunted hare . . . it's always the same, the same!

'Wait!' I think, 'I will cheat her! I will go nowhere!' and I instantly sat down on the ground.

The old woman stands behind, two paces from me. I do not hear her, but I feel she is there.

And suddenly I see the blur of darkness in the distance is floating, creeping of itself towards me!

God! I look round again . . . the old woman looks straight at me, and her toothless mouth is twisted in a grin.

No escape!

THE DOG

Us two in the room; my dog and me. . . . Outside a fearful storm is howling.

The dog sits in front of me, and looks me straight in the face.

And I, too, look into his face.

He wants, it seems, to tell me something. He is dumb, he is without words, he does not understand himself—but I understand him.

I understand that at this instant there is living in him and in me the same feeling, that there is no difference between us. We are the same; in each of us there burns and shines the same trembling spark.

Death sweeps down, with a wave of its chill broad wing. . . .

And the end!

Who then can discern what was the spark that glowed in each of us?

No! We are not beast and man that glance at one another. . . .

They are the eyes of equals, those eyes riveted on one another.

And in each of these, in the beast and in the man, the same life huddles up in fear close to the other.

February 1878.

MY ADVERSARY

I HAD a comrade who was my adversary; not in pursuits, nor in service, nor in love, but our views were never alike on any subject, and whenever we met, endless argument arose between us.

We argued about everything: about art, and religion, and science, about life on earth and beyond the grave, especially about life beyond the grave.

He was a person of faith and enthusiasm. One day he said to me, 'You laugh at every-thing; but if I die before you, I will come to you from the other world. . . . We shall see whether you will laugh then.'

And he did, in fact, die before me, while he was still young; but the years went by, and I had forgotten his promise, his threat.

One night I was lying in bed, and could not, and, indeed, would not sleep.

In the room it was neither dark nor light. I fell to staring into the grey twilight.

And all at once, I fancied that between the two windows my adversary was standing, and was slowly and mournfully nodding his head up and down.

I was not frightened; I was not even surprised . . . but raising myself a little, and propping myself on my elbow, I stared still more intently at the unexpected apparition.

The latter continued to nod his head.

'Well?' I said at last; 'are you triumphant or regretful? What is this—warning or reproach? . . . Or do you mean to give me to understand that you were wrong, that we were both wrong? What are you experiencing? The torments of hell? Or the bliss of paradise? Utter one word at least!'

But my opponent did not utter a single sound, and only, as before, mournfully and submissively nodded his head up and down.

I laughed . . . he vanished.

February 1878.

THE BEGGAR

I WAS walking along the street . . . I was stopped by a decrepit old beggar.

Bloodshot, tearful eyes, blue lips, coarse rags, festering wounds. . . . Oh, how hideously poverty had eaten into this miserable creature!

He held out to me a red, swollen, filthy hand. He groaned, he mumbled of help.

I began feeling in all my pockets. . . . No purse, no watch, not even a handkerchief. . . . I had taken nothing with me. And the beggar was still waiting . . . and his outstretched hand feebly shook and trembled.

Confused, abashed, I warmly clasped the filthy, shaking hand . . . 'Don't be angry, brother; I have nothing, brother.'

The beggar stared at me with his bloodshot eyes; his blue lips smiled; and he in his turn gripped my chilly fingers.

'What of it, brother?' he mumbled; 'thanks for this, too. That is a gift too, brother.'

I knew that I too had received a gift from my brother.

February 1878.

'THOU SHALT HEAR THE FOOL'S JUDG-
MENT . . .' —*PUSHKIN*

'THOU shalt hear the fool's judgment . . . .'
You always told the truth, O great singer of
ours. You spoke it this time, too.

'The fool's judgment and the laughter of the
crowd' . . . who has not known the one and the
other?

All that one can, and one ought to bear;
and who has the strength, let him despise it!

But there are blows which pierce more cruelly
to the very heart. . . . A man has done all that
he could; has worked strenuously, lovingly,
honestly. . . . And honest hearts turn from him
in disgust; honest faces burn with indignation
at his name. 'Be gone! Away with you!'
honest young voices scream at him. 'We have
no need of you, nor of your work. You pollute
our dwelling-places. You know us not and
understand us not. . . . You are our enemy!'

What is that man to do? Go on working;
not try to justify himself, and not even look
forward to a fairer judgment

At one time the tillers of the soil cursed the
traveller who brought the potato, the substitute
for bread, the poor man's daily food. . . . They

shook the precious gift out of his outstretched hands, flung it in the mud, trampled it underfoot.

Now they are fed with it, and do not even know their benefactor's name.

So be it! What is his name to them? He, nameless though he be, saves them from hunger.

Let us try only that what we bring should be really good food.

Bitter, unjust reproach on the lips of those you love. . . . But that, too, can be borne. . . .

'Beat me! but listen!' said the Athenian leader to the Spartan.

'Beat me! but be healthy and fed!' we ought to say.

February 1878.

A CONTENTED MAN

A YOUNG man goes skipping and bounding along a street in the capital. His movements are gay and alert; there is a sparkle in his eyes, a smirk on his lips, a pleasing flush on his beaming face. . . . He is all contentment and delight.

What has happened to him? Has he come

in for a legacy? Has he been promoted? Is he hastening to meet his beloved? Or is it simply he has had a good breakfast, and the sense of health, the sense of well-fed prosperity, is at work in all his limbs? Surely they have not put on his neck thy lovely, eight-pointed cross, O Polish king, Stanislas?

No. He has hatched a scandal against a friend, has sedulously sown it abroad, has heard it, this same slander, from the lips of another friend, and — *has himself believed it!*

Oh, how contented! how kind indeed at this minute is this amiable, promising young man!

February 1878.

A RULE OF LIFE

'If you want to annoy an opponent thoroughly, and even to harm him,' said a crafty old knave to me, 'you reproach him with the very defect or vice you are conscious of in yourself. Be indignant . . . and reproach him!

'To begin with, it will set others thinking you have not that vice.

'In the second place, your indignation may well be sincere . . . You can turn to account the pricks of your own conscience.

If you, for instance, are a turncoat, reproach your opponent with having no convictions!

'If you are yourself slavish at heart, tell him reproachfully that he is slavish . . . the slave of civilisation, of Europe, of Socialism!'

'One might even say, the slave of anti-slavishness,' I suggested.

'You might even do that,' assented the cunning knave.

February 1878.

THE END OF THE WORLD

A DREAM

I FANCIED I was somewhere in Russia, in the wilds, in a simple country house.

The room big and low pitched with three windows; the walls whitewashed; no furniture. Before the house a barren plain; gradually sloping downwards, it stretches into the distance; a grey monotonous sky hangs over it, like the canopy of a bed.

I am not alone; there are some ten persons in the room with me. All quite plain people, simply dressed. They walk up and down in silence, as it were stealthily. They avoid one another, and yet are continually looking anxiously at one another.

Not one knows why he has come into this house and what people there are with him. On all the faces uneasiness and despondency . . . all in turn approach the windows and look about intently as though expecting something from without.

Then again they fall to wandering up and down. Among us is a small-sized boy; from time to time he whimpers in the same thin voice, 'Father, I'm frightened!' My heart turns sick at his whimper, and I too begin to be afraid . . . of what? I don't know myself. Only I feel, there is coming nearer and nearer a great, great calamity.

The boy keeps on and on with his wail. Oh, to escape from here! How stifling! How weary! how heavy. . . . But escape is impossible.

That sky is like a shroud. And no wind. . . . Is the air dead or what?

All at once the boy runs up to the window and shrieks in the same piteous voice, 'Look! look! the earth has fallen away!'

'How? fallen away?' Yes; just now there was a plain before the house, and now it stands on a fearful height! The horizon has sunk, has gone down, and from the very house drops an

255

almost overhanging, as it were scooped-out, black precipice.

We all crowded to the window. . . . Horror froze our hearts. 'Here it is . . . here it is!' whispers one next me.

And behold, along the whole far boundary of the earth, something began to stir, some sort of small, roundish hillocks began heaving and falling.

'It is the sea!' the thought flashed on us all at the same instant. 'It will swallow us all up directly. . . . Only how can it grow and rise upwards? To this precipice?'

And yet, it grows, grows enormously. . . . Already there are not separate hillocks heaving in the distance. . . . One continuous, monstrous wave embraces the whole circle of the horizon.

It is swooping, swooping, down upon us! In an icy hurricane it flies, swirling in the darkness of hell. Everything shuddered—and there, in this flying mass—was the crash of thunder, the iron wail of thousands of throats. . . .

Ah! what a roaring and moaning! It was the earth howling for terror. . . .

The end of it! the end of all!

The child whimpered once more. . . . I tried to clutch at my companions, but already we were all crushed, buried, drowned, swept away by that pitch-black, icy, thundering wave!

Darkness . . . darkness everlasting!
Scarcely breathing, I awoke.

March 1878.

MASHA

WHEN I lived, many years ago, in Petersburg, every time I chanced to hire a sledge, I used to get into conversation with the driver.

I was particularly fond of talking to the night drivers, poor peasants from the country round, who come to the capital with their little ochre-painted sledges and wretched nags, in the hope of earning food for themselves and rent for their masters.

So one day I engaged such a sledge-driver. . . . He was a lad of twenty, tall and well-made, a splendid fellow with blue eyes and ruddy cheeks; his fair hair curled in little ringlets under the shabby little patched cap that was pulled over his eyes. And how had that little torn smock ever been drawn over those gigantic shoulders!

But the handsome, beardless face of the sledge-driver looked mournful and downcast.

I began to talk to him. There was a sorrowful note in his voice too.

'What is it, brother?' I asked him; 'why aren't you cheerful? Have you some trouble?'

The lad did not answer me for a minute. 'Yes, sir, I have,' he said at last. 'And such a trouble, there could not be a worse. My wife is dead.'

'You loved her . . . your wife?'

The lad did not turn to me; he only bent his head a little.

'I loved her, sir. It's eight months since then . . . but I can't forget it. My heart is gnawing at me . . . so it is! And why had she to die? A young thing! strong! . . . In one day cholera snatched her away.'

'And was she good to you?'

'Ah, sir!' the poor fellow sighed heavily, 'and how happy we were together! She died without me! The first I heard here, they'd buried her already, you know; I hurried off at once to the village, home—I got there—it was past midnight I went into my hut, stood still in the middle of the room, and softly I whispered, "Masha! eh, Masha!" Nothing but the cricket chirping. I fell a-crying then, sat on the hut floor, and beat on the earth with my fists! "Greedy earth!" says I . . . "You have swallowed her up . . . swallow me too!— Ah, Masha!"

'Masha!' be added suddenly in a sinking

voice. And without letting go of the cord reins, he wiped the tears out of his eyes with his sleeve, shook it, shrugged his shoulders, and uttered not another word.

As I got out of the sledge, I gave him a few coppers over his fare. He bowed low to me, grasping his cap in both hands, and drove off at a walking pace over the level snow of the deserted street, full of the grey fog of a January frost.

April 1878.

THE FOOL

THERE lived a fool.

For a long time he lived in peace and contentment; but by degrees rumours began to reach him that he was regarded on all sides as a vulgar idiot.

The fool was abashed and began to ponder gloomily how he might put an end to these unpleasant rumours.

A sudden idea, at last, illuminated his dull little brain . . . And, without the slightest delay, he put it into practice.

A friend met him in the street, and fell to praising a well-known painter . . . .

'Upon my word!' cried the fool, 'that painter was out of date long ago . . . you didn't know it? I should never have expected it of you . . . you are quite behind the times.'

The friend was alarmed, and promptly agreed with the fool.

'Such a splendid book I read yesterday!' said another friend to him.

'Upon my word!' cried the fool, 'I wonder you're not ashamed. That book's good for nothing; every one's seen through it long ago. Didn't you know it? You're quite behind the times.'

This friend too was alarmed, and he agreed with the fool.

'What a wonderful fellow my friend N. N. is!' said a third friend to the fool. 'Now there's a really generous creature!'

'Upon my word!' cried the fool. 'N. N., the notorious scoundrel! He swindled all his relations. Every one knows that. You're quite behind the times.'

The third friend too was alarmed, and he agreed with the fool and deserted his friend. And whoever and whatever was praised in the fool's presence, he had the same retort for everything.

Sometimes he would add reproachfully: 'And do you still believe in authorities?'

'Spiteful! malignant!' his friends began to say of the fool. 'But what a brain!'

'And what a tongue!' others would add, 'Oh, yes, he has talent!'

It ended in the editor of a journal proposing to the fool that he should undertake their reviewing column.

And the fool fell to criticising everything and every one, without in the least changing his manner, or his exclamations.

Now he, who once declaimed against authorities, is himself an authority, and the young men venerate him, and fear him.

And what else can they do, poor young men? Though one ought not, as a general rule, to venerate any one . . . but in this case, if one didn't venerate him, one would find oneself quite behind the times!

Fools have a good time among cowards.

April 1878.

AN EASTERN LEGEND

WHO in Bagdad knows not Jaffar, the Sun of the Universe?

One day, many years ago (he was yet a youth), Jaffar was walking in the environs of Bagdad.

Suddenly a hoarse cry reached his ear; some one was calling desperately for help.

Jaffar was distinguished among the young men of his age by prudence and sagacity; but his heart was compassionate, and he relied on his strength.

He ran at the cry, and saw an infirm old man, pinned to the city wall by two brigands, who were robbing him.

Jaffar drew his sabre and fell upon the miscreants: one he killed, the other he drove away.

The old man thus liberated fell at his deliverer's feet, and, kissing the hem of his garment, cried: 'Valiant youth, your magnanimity shall not remain unrewarded. In appearance I am a poor beggar; but only in appearance. I am not a common man. Come to-morrow in the early morning to the chief bazaar; I will await you at the fountain, and you shall be convinced of the truth of my words.

Jaffar thought: 'In appearance this man is a beggar, certainly; but all sorts of things happen. Why not put it to the test?' and he answered: 'Very well, good father; I will come.'

The old man looked into his face, and went away.

The next morning, the sun had hardly risen, Jaffar went to the bazaar. The old man was already awaiting him, leaning with his elbow on the marble basin of the fountain.

In silence he took Jaffar by the hand and led him into a small garden, enclosed on all sides by high walls.

In the very middle of this garden, on a green lawn, grew an extraordinary-looking tree.

It was like a cypress; only its leaves were of an azure hue.

Three fruits—three apples—hung on the slender upward-bent twigs; one was of middle size, long-shaped, and milk-white; the second, large, round, bright-red; the third, small, wrinkled, yellowish.

The whole tree faintly rustled, though there was no wind. It emitted a shrill plaintive ringing sound, as of a glass bell; it seemed it was conscious of Jaffar's approach.

'Youth!' said the old man, 'pick any one of these apples and know, if you pick and eat the white one, you will be the wisest of all men; if you pick and eat the red, you will be rich as the Jew Rothschild; if you pick and eat the yellow one, you will be liked by old women. Make up your mind! and do not delay. Within an hour the apples will wither, and the tree itself will sink into the dumb depths of the earth!'

Jaffar looked down, and pondered. 'How

am I to act? 'he said in an undertone, as though arguing with himself.' If you become too wise, maybe you will not care to live; if you become richer than any one, every one will envy you; I had better pick and eat the third, the withered apple!'

And so he did; and the old man laughed a toothless laugh, and said: 'O wise young man! You have chosen the better part! What need have you of the white apple? You are wiser than Solomon as it is. And you've no need of the red apple either. . . . You will be rich without it Only your wealth no one will envy.'

'Tell me, old man,' said Jaffar, rousing himself, 'where lives the honoured mother of our Caliph, protected of heaven?'

The old man bowed down to the earth, and pointed out to the young man the way.

Who in Bagdad knows not the Sun of the Universe, the great, the renowned Jaffar?

April 1878.

TWO STANZAS

THERE was once a town, the inhabitants of which were so passionately fond of poetry, that if some weeks passed by without the appearance of any good new poems, they regarded such a poetic dearth as a public misfortune.

They used at such times to put on their worst clothes, to sprinkle ashes on their heads; and, assembling in crowds in the public squares, to shed tears and bitterly to upbraid the muse who had deserted them.

On one such inauspicious day, the young poet Junius came into a square, thronged with the grieving populace.

With rapid steps he ascended a forum constructed for this purpose, and made signs that he wished to recite a poem.

The lictors at once brandished their fasces. 'Silence! attention!' they shouted loudly, and the crowd was hushed in expectation.

'Friends! Comrades!' began Junius, in a loud but not quite steady voice:—

'Friends! Comrades! Lovers of the Muse!
Ye worshippers of beauty and of grace!
Let not a moment's gloom dismay your souls,
Your heart's desire is nigh, and light shall banish darkness.'

Junius ceased . . . and in answer to him, from every part of the square, rose a hubbub of hissing and laughter.

Every face, turned to him, glowed with indignation, every eye sparkled with anger, every arm was raised and shook a menacing fist!

'He thought to dazzle us with that!' growled angry voices. 'Down with the imbecile rhyme-ster from the forum! Away with the idiot! Rotten apples, stinking eggs for the motley fool! Give us stones—stones here!'

Junius rushed head over heels from the forum . . . but, before he had got home, he was over-taken by the sound of peals of enthusiastic applause, cries and shouts of admiration.

Filled with amazement, Junius returned to the square, trying however to avoid being noticed (for it is dangerous to irritate an in-furiated beast).

And what did he behold?

High above the people, upon their shoulders, on a flat golden shield, wrapped in a purple chlamys, with a laurel wreath on his flowing locks, stood his rival, the young poet Julius. . . . And the populace all round him shouted: 'Glory! Glory! Glory to the immortal Julius! He has comforted us in our sorrow, in our great woe! He has bestowed on us verses sweeter than honey, more musical than the cymbal's note, more fragrant than the rose, purer than the azure of heaven! Carry him in triumph, encircle his inspired head with the soft breath of incense, cool his brow with the rhythmic movement of palm-leaves, scatter at his feet all the fragrance of the myrrh of Arabia! Glory!'

Junius went up to one of the applauding enthusiasts. 'Enlighten me, O my fellow-citizen! what were the verses with which Julius has made you happy? I, alas! was not in the square when he uttered them! Repeat them, if you remember them, pray!'

'Verses like those I could hardly forget!' the man addressed responded with spirit 'What do you take me for? Listen—and rejoice, rejoice with us!'

'Lovers of the Muse!' so the deified Julius had begun . . . .

'Lovers of the Muse! Comrades! Friends
Of beauty, grace, and music, worshippers!
Let not your hearts by gloom affrighted be!
The wished-for moment comes! and day shall scatter night!'

'What do you think of them?'

'Heavens!' cried Junius; 'but that's my poem! Julius must have been in the crowd when I was reciting them; he heard them and repeated them, slightly varying, and certainly not improving, a few expressions.'

'Aha! Now I recognise you. . . . You are Junius,' the citizen he had stopped retorted with a scowl on his face. 'Envious man or fool! . . . note only, luckless wretch, how sublimely Julius has phrased it: "And day shall scatter night!" While you had some such

rubbish: "And light shall banish darkness!"
What light? What darkness?'

'But isn't that just the same?' Junius was
beginning . . . .

'Say another word,' the citizen cut him short,
'I will call upon the people . . . they will tear
you to pieces!'

Junius judiciously held his peace, but a grey-
headed old man who had heard the conversation went up to the unlucky poet, and laying a
hand upon his shoulder, said:

'Junius! You uttered your own thought, but
not at the right moment; and he uttered not
his own thought, but at the right moment.
Consequently, he is all right; while for you is
left the consolations of a good conscience.'

But while his conscience, to the best of its
powers—not over successfully, to tell the truth
—was consoling Junius as he was shoved on
one side—in the distance, amid shouts of
applause and rejoicing, in the golden radiance
of the all-conquering sun, resplendent in purple,
with his brow shaded with laurel, among undulating clouds of lavish incense, with majestic
deliberation, like a tsar making a triumphal
entry into his kingdom, moved the proudly erect
figure of Julius . . . and the long branches of
palm rose and fell before him, as though ex-
pressing in their soft vibration, in their sub-

missive obeisance, the ever-renewed adoration which filled the hearts of his enchanted fellow-citizens!

April 1878.

THE SPARROW

I WAS returning from hunting, and walking along an avenue of the garden, my dog running in front of me.

Suddenly he took shorter steps, and began to steal along as though tracking game.

I looked along the avenue, and saw a young sparrow, with yellow about its beak and down on its head. It had fallen out of the nest (the wind was violently shaking the birch-trees in the avenue) and sat unable to move, helplessly flapping its half-grown wings.

My dog was slowly approaching it, when, suddenly darting down from a tree close by, an old dark-throated sparrow fell like a stone right before his nose, and all ruffled up, terrified, with despairing and pitiful cheeps, it flung itself twice towards the open jaws of shining teeth.

It sprang to save; it cast itself before its nestling . . . but all its tiny body was shaking with terror; its note was harsh and strange. Swooning with fear, it offered itself up!

What a huge monster must the dog have seemed to it! And yet it could not stay on its high branch out of danger. . . . A force stronger than its will flung it down.

My Trésor stood still, drew back. . . . Clearly he too recognised this force.

I hastened to call off the disconcerted dog, and went away, full of reverence.

Yes; do not laugh. I felt reverence for that tiny heroic bird, for its impulse of love.

Love, I thought, is stronger than death or the fear of death. Only by it, by love, life holds together and advances.

April 1878.

THE SKULLS

A SUMPTUOUS, brilliantly lighted hall; a number of ladies and gentlemen.

All the faces are animated, the talk is lively. . . . A noisy conversation is being carried on about a famous singer. They call her divine, immortal. . . . O, how finely yesterday she rendered her last trill!

And suddenly—as by the wave of an enchanter's wand—from every head and from every face, slipped off the delicate covering of skin, and instantaneously exposed the deadly whiteness of skulls, with here and there the leaden shimmer of bare jaws and gums.

With horror I beheld the movements of those jaws and gums; the turning, the glistening in the light of the lamps and candles, of those lumpy bony balls, and the rolling in them of other smaller balls, the balls of the meaningless eyes.

I dared not touch my own face, dared not glance at myself in the glass.

And the skulls turned from side to side as before. . . . And with their former noise, peeping like little red rags out of the grinning teeth, rapid tongues lisped how marvellously, how inimitably the immortal . . . yes, immortal . . . singer had rendered that last trill!

April 1878.

THE WORKMAN AND THE MAN WITH WHITE HANDS

A DIALOGUE

WORKMAN. Why do you come crawling up to us? What do ye want? You're none of us. . . . Get along!

MAN WITH WHITE HANDS. I am one of you, comrades!

THE WORKMAN. One of us, indeed! That's a notion! Look at my hands. D'ye see how dirty they are? And they smell of muck, and of pitch—but yours, see, are white. And what do they smell of?

THE MAN WITH WHITE HANDS (*offering his hands*). Smell them.

THE WORKMAN (*sniffing his hands*). That's a queer start. Seems like a smell of iron.

THE MAN WITH WHITE HANDS. Yes; iron it is. For six long years I wore chains on them.

THE WORKMAN. And what was that for, pray?

THE MAN WITH WHITE HANDS. Why, because I worked for your good; tried to set free the oppressed and the ignorant; stirred folks up against your oppressors; resisted the authorities. . . . So they locked me up.

THE WORKMAN. Locked you up, did they? Serve you right for resisting!

Two Years Later.

THE SAME WORKMAN TO ANOTHER. I say, Pete. . . . Do you remember, the year before last, a chap with white hands talking to you?

272

THE OTHER WORKMAN. Yes; . . . what of it?

THE fiRST WORKMAN. They're going to hang him to-day, I heard say; that's the order.

THE SECOND WORKMAN. Did he keep on resisting the authorities?

THE fiRST WORKMAN. He kept on.

THE SECOND WORKMAN. Ah! . . . Now, I say, mate, couldn't we get hold of a bit of the rope they're going to hang him with? They do say, it brings good luck to a house!

THE fiRST WORKMAN. You're right there. We'll have a try for it, mate.

April 1878.

THE ROSE

THE last days of August. . . . Autumn was already at hand.

The sun was setting. A sudden downpour of rain, without thunder or lightning, had just passed rapidly over our wide plain.

The garden in front of the house glowed and steamed, all filled with the fire of the sunset and the deluge of rain.

She was sitting at a table in the drawing-

273

room, and, with persistent dreaminess, gazing through the half-open door into the garden.

I knew what was passing at that moment in her soul; I knew that, after a brief but agonising struggle, she was at that instant giving herself up to a feeling she could no longer master.

All at once she got up, went quickly out into the garden, and disappeared.

An hour passed . . . a second; she had not returned.

Then I got up, and, getting out of the house, I turned along the walk by which—of that I had no doubt—she had gone.

All was darkness about me; the night had already fallen. But on the damp sand of the path a roundish object could be discerned— bright red even through the mist

I stooped down. It was a fresh, new-blown rose. Two hours before I had seen this very rose on her bosom.

I carefully picked up the flower that had fallen in the mud, and, going back to the drawing-room, laid it on the table before her chair.

And now at last she came back, and with light footsteps, crossing the whole room, sat down at the table.

Her face was both paler and more vivid; her

downcast eyes, that looked somehow smaller, strayed rapidly in happy confusion from side to side.

She saw the rose, snatched it up, glanced at its crushed, muddy petals, glanced at me, and her eyes, brought suddenly to a standstill, were bright with tears.

'What are you crying for?' I asked.

'Why, see this rose. Look what has happened to it.'

Then I thought fit to utter a profound remark.

'Your tears will wash away the mud,' I pronounced with a significant expression.

'Tears do not wash, they burn,' she answered. And turning to the hearth she flung the rose into the dying flame.

'Fire burns even better than tears,' she cried with spirit; and her lovely eyes, still bright with tears, laughed boldly and happily.

I saw that she too had been in the fire.

April 1878.

TO THE MEMORY OF U. P. VREVSKY

ON dirt, on stinking wet straw under the shelter of a tumble-down barn, turned in haste into a camp hospital, in a ruined Bulgarian village, for over a fortnight she lay dying of typhus.

She was unconscious, and not one doctor even looked at her; the sick soldiers, whom she had tended as long as she could keep on her legs, in their turn got up from their pestilent litters to lift a few drops of water in the hollow of a broken pot to her parched lips.

She was young and beautiful; the great world knew her; even the highest dignitaries had been interested in her. Ladies had envied her, men had paid her court . . . two or three had loved her secretly and truly. Life had smiled on her; but there are smiles that are worse than tears.

A soft, tender heart . . . and such force, such eagerness for sacrifice! To help those who needed help . . . she knew of no other happiness . . . knew not of it, and had never once known it Every other happiness passed her by. But she had long made up her mind to that; and all aglow with the fire of unquench- able faith, she gave herself to the service of her neighbours.

What hidden treasure she buried there in the depth of her heart, in her most secret soul, no one ever knew; and now, of course, no one will ever know.

Ay, and what need? Her sacrifice is made . . . her work is done.

But grievous it is to think that no one said thanks even to her dead body, though she herself was shy and shrank from all thanks.

May her dear shade pardon this belated blossom, which I make bold to lay upon her grave!

September 1878.

THE LAST MEETING

WE had once been close and warm friends. . . . But an unlucky moment came . . . and we parted as enemies.

Many years passed by. . . . And coming to the town where he lived, I learnt that he was helplessly ill, and wished to see me.

I made my way to him, went into his room. . . . Our eyes met.

I hardly knew him. God! what sickness had done to him!

Yellow, wrinkled, completely bald, with a scanty grey beard, he sat clothed in nothing but a shirt purposely slit open. . . . He could not bear the weight of even the lightest clothes. Jerkily he stretched out to me his fearfully thin hand that looked as if it were gnawed away, with an effort muttered a few indistinct words— whether of welcome or reproach, who can tell? His emaciated chest heaved, and over the dwindled pupils of his kindling eyes rolled two hard-wrung tears of suffering.

My heart sank. . . . I sat down on a chair beside him, and involuntarily dropping my eyes before the horror and hideousness of it, I too held out my hand.

But it seemed to me that it was not his hand that took hold of me.

It seemed to me that between us is sitting a tall, still, white woman. A long robe shrouds her from head to foot. Her deep, pale eyes look into vacancy; no sound is uttered by her pale, stern lips.

This woman has joined our hands. . . . She has reconciled us for ever.

Yes. . . . Death has reconciled us. . . .

April 1878.

A VISIT

I was sitting at the open window . . . in the morning, the early morning of the first of May. The dawn had not yet begun; but already the dark, warm night grew pale and chill at its approach.

No mist had risen, no breeze was astir, all was colourless and still . . . but the nearness of the awakening could be felt, and the rarer air smelt keen and moist with dew.

Suddenly, at the open window, with a light whirr and rustle, a great bird flew into my room.

I started, looked closely at it. . . . It was not a bird; it was a tiny winged woman, dressed in a narrow long robe flowing to her feet.

She was grey all over, the colour of mother-of-pearl; only the inner side of her wings glowed with the tender flush of an opening rose; a wreath of valley lilies entwined the scattered curls upon her little round head; and, like a butterfly's feelers, two peacock feathers waved drolly above her lovely rounded brow.

She fluttered twice about the ceiling; her tiny face was laughing; laughing, too, were her great, clear, black eyes.

The gay frolic of her sportive flight set them flashing like diamonds.

She held in her hand the long stalk of a flower of the steppes—'the Tsar's sceptre,' the Russians call it—it is really like a sceptre.

Flying rapidly above me, she touched my head with the flower.

279

I rushed towards her. . . . But already she had fluttered out of window, and darted away....

In the garden, in a thicket of lilac bushes, a wood-dove greeted her with its first morning warble . . . and where she vanished, the milk-white sky flushed a soft pink.

I know thee, Goddess of Fantasy! Thou didst pay me a random visit by the way; thou hast flown on to the young poets.

O Poesy! Youth! Virginal beauty of woman! Thou couldst shine for me but for a moment, in the early dawn of early spring!

May 1878.

NECESSITAS — VIS — LIBERTAS!

A BAS-RELIEF

A TALL, bony old woman, with iron face and dull, fixed look, moves with long strides, and, with an arm dry as a stick, pushes before her another woman.

This woman—of huge stature, powerful, thick-set, with the muscles of a Hercules, with a tiny head set on a bull neck, and blind—in her turn pushes before her a small, thin girl.

280

This girl alone has eyes that see; she resists, turns round, lifts fair, delicate hands; her face, full of life, shows impatience and daring. . . . She wants not to obey, she wants not to go, where they are driving her . . . but, still, she has to yield and go.

Necessitas—Vis—Libertas!

Who will, may translate.

May 1878.

ALMS

NEAR a large town, along the broad highroad walked an old sick man.

He tottered as he went; his old wasted legs, halting, dragging, stumbling, moved painfully and feebly, as though they did not belong to him; his clothes hung in rags about him; his uncovered head drooped on his breast. . . . He was utterly worn-out.

He sat down on a stone by the wayside, bent forward, leant his elbows on his knees, hid his face in his hands; and through the knotted fingers the tears dropped down on to the grey, dry dust.

He remembered. . . .

Remembered how he too had been strong

and rich, and how he had wasted his health, and had lavished his riches upon others, friends and enemies. . . . And here, he had not now a crust of bread; and all had forsaken him, friends even before foes. . . . Must he sink to begging alms? There was bitterness in his heart, and shame.

The tears still dropped and dropped, spotting the grey dust.

Suddenly he heard some one call him by his name; he lifted his weary head, and saw standing before him a stranger.

A face calm and grave, but not stern; eyes not beaming, but clear; a look penetrating, but not unkind.

'Thou hast given away all thy riches,' said a tranquil voice. . . . 'But thou dost not regret having done good, surely?'

'I regret it not,' answered the old man with a sigh; 'but here I am dying now.'

'And had there been no beggars who held out their hands to thee,' the stranger went on, 'thou wouldst have had none on whom to prove thy goodness; thou couldst not have done thy good works.'

The old man answered nothing, and pondered.

'So be thou also now not proud, poor man,' the stranger began again. 'Go thou, hold out thy hand; do thou too give to other good men a chance to prove in deeds that they are good.'

The old man started, raised his eyes . . . but already the stranger had vanished, and in the distance a man came into sight walking along the road.

The old man went up to him, and held out his hand. This man turned away with a surly face, and gave him nothing.

But after him another passed, and he gave the old man some trifling alms.

And the old man bought himself bread with the coppers given him, and sweet to him seemed the morsel gained by begging, and there was no shame in his heart, but the contrary: peace and joy came as a blessing upon him.

May 1878.

THE INSECT

I DREAMED that we were sitting, a party of twenty, in a big room with open windows.

Among us were women, children, old men. . . . We were all talking of some very well-known subject, talking noisily and indistinctly.

Suddenly, with a sharp, whirring sound, there

flew into the room a big insect, two inches long
. . . it flew in, circled round, and settled on the
wall.

It was like a fly or a wasp. Its body dirt-
coloured; of the same colour too its flat, stiff
wings; outspread feathered claws, and a head
thick and angular, like a dragon-fly's; both
head and claws were bright red, as though
steeped in blood.

This strange insect incessantly turned its
head up and down, to right and to left, moved
its claws . . . then suddenly darted from the
wall, flew with a whirring sound about the
room, and again settled, again hatefully and
loathsomely wriggling all over, without stirring
from the spot.

In all of us it excited a sensation of loathing,
dread, even terror. . . . No one of us had ever
seen anything like it. We all cried: 'Drive
that monstrous thing away!' and waved our
handkerchiefs at it from a distance . . . but no
one ventured to go up to it . . . and when the
insect began flying, every one instinctively
moved away.

Only one of our party, a pale-faced young
man, stared at us all in amazement. He
shrugged his shoulders; he smiled, and positively could not conceive what had happened
to us, and why we were in such a state of

excitement. He himself did not see an insect at all, did not hear the ill-omened whirr of its wings.

All at once the insect seemed to stare at him, darted off, and dropping on his head, stung him on the forehead, above the eyes. . . . The young man feebly groaned, and fell dead.

The fearful fly flew out at once. . . . Only then we guessed what it was had visited us.

May 1878.

CABBAGE SOUP

A PEASANT woman, a widow, had an only son, a young man of twenty, the best workman in the village, and he died.

The lady who was the owner of the village, hearing of the woman's trouble, went to visit her on the very day of the burial.

She found her at home.

Standing in the middle of her hut, before the table, she was, without haste, with a regular movement of the right arm (the left hung listless at her side), scooping up weak cabbage soup from the bottom of a blackened pot, and swallowing it spoonful by spoonful.

The woman's face was sunken and dark; her eyes were red and swollen . . . but she held herself as rigid and upright as in church.

'Heavens!' thought the lady, 'she can eat at such a moment . . . what coarse feelings they have really, all of them!'

And at that point the lady recollected that when, a few years before, she had lost her little daughter, nine months old, she had refused, in her grief, a lovely country villa near Petersburg, and had spent the whole summer in town! Meanwhile the woman went on swallowing cabbage soup.

The lady could not contain herself, at last 'Tatiana!' she said . . . 'Really! I'm surprised! Is it possible you didn't care for your son? How is it you've not lost your appetite? How can you eat that soup!'

'My Vasia's dead,' said the woman quietly, and tears of anguish ran once more down her hollow cheeks. 'It's the end of me too, of course; it's tearing the heart out of me alive. But the soup's not to be wasted; there's salt in it'

The lady only shrugged her shoulders and went away. Salt did not cost her much.

May 1878.

THE REALM OF AZURE

O REALM of azure! O realm of light and colour, of youth and happiness! I have beheld thee in dream. We were together, a few, in a beautiful little boat, gaily decked out. Like a swan's breast the white sail swelled below the streamers frolicking in the wind.

I knew not who were with me; but in all my soul I felt that they were young, light-hearted, happy as I!

But I looked not indeed on them. I beheld all round the boundless blue of the sea, dimpled with scales of gold, and overhead the same boundless sea of blue, and in it, triumphant and mirthful, it seemed, moved the sun.

And among us, ever and anon, rose laughter, ringing and gleeful as the laughter of the gods!

And on a sudden, from one man's lips or another's, would flow words, songs of divine beauty and inspiration, and power . . . it seemed the sky itself echoed back a greeting to them, and the sea quivered in unison. . . . Then followed again the blissful stillness.

Riding lightly over the soft waves, swiftly our little boat sped on. No wind drove it along; our own lightly beating hearts guided it At our will it floated, obedient as a living thing.

We came on islands, enchanted islands, half-transparent with the prismatic lights of precious stones, of amethysts and emeralds. Odours of bewildering fragrance rose from the rounded shores; some of these islands showered on us a rain of roses and valley lilies; from others birds darted up, with long wings of rainbow hues.

The birds flew circling above us; the lilies and roses melted away in the pearly foam that glided by the smooth sides of our boat.

And, with the flowers and the birds, sounds floated to us, sounds sweet as honey . . . women's voices, one fancied, in them. . . . And all about us, sky, sea, the heaving sail aloft, the gurgling water at the rudder—all spoke of love, of happy love!

And she, the beloved of each of us—she was there . . . unseen and close. One moment more, and behold, her eyes will shine upon thee, her smile will blossom on thee . . . Her hand will take thy hand and guide thee to the land of joy that fades not!

O realm of azure! In dream have I beheld thee.

June 1878.

TWO RICH MEN

WHEN I hear the praises of the rich man Rothschild, who out of his immense revenues devotes whole thousands to the education of children, the care of the sick, the support of the aged, I admire and am touched.

But even while I admire it and am touched by it, I cannot help recalling a poor peasant family who took an orphan niece into their little tumble-down hut.

'If we take Katka,' said the woman,' our last farthing will go on her, there won't be enough to get us salt to salt us a bit of bread.'

'Well, . . . we'll do without salt,' answered the peasant, her husband.

Rothschild is a long way behind that peasant!

July 1878.

THE OLD MAN

DAYS of darkness, of dreariness, have come. . . . Thy own infirmities, the sufferings of those dear to thee, the chill and gloom of old age. All that thou hast loved, to which thou hast given

thyself irrevocably, is falling, going to pieces.
The way is all down-hill.

What canst thou do? Grieve? Complain?
Thou wilt aid not thyself nor others that way. . . .

On the bowed and withering tree the leaves
are smaller and fewer, but its green is yet the
same.

Do thou too shrink within, withdraw into
thyself, into thy memories, and there, deep
down, in the very depths of the soul turned
inwards on itself, thy old life, to which thou
alone hast the key, will be bright again for
thee, in all the fragrance, all the fresh green,
and the grace and power of its spring!

But beware . . . look not forward, poor old
man!

July 1878.

THE REPORTER

Two friends were sitting at a table drinking
tea.

A sudden hubbub arose in the street They
heard pitiable groans, furious abuse, bursts of
malignant laughter.

'They're beating some one,' observed one of
the friends, looking out of window.

'A criminal? A murderer?' inquired the other. 'I say, whatever he may be, we can't allow this illegal chastisement. Let's go and take his part.'

'But it's not a murderer they're beating.'

'Not a murderer? Is it a thief then? It makes no difference, let's go and get him away from the crowd.'

'It's not a thief either.'

'Not a thief? Is it an absconding cashier then, a railway director, an army contractor, a Russian art patron, a lawyer, a Conservative editor, a social reformer? . . . Any way, let's go and help him!'

'No . . . it's a newspaper reporter they're beating.'

'A reporter? Oh, I. tell you what: we'll finish our glasses of tea first then.'

July 1878.

THE TWO BROTHERS

IT was a vision . . .

Two angels appeared to me . . . two genii.

I say angels, genii, because both had no clothes on their naked bodies, and behind their shoulders rose long powerful wings.

Both were youths. One was rather plump, with soft smooth skin and dark curls. His eyes were brown and full, with thick eyelashes; his look was sly, merry, and eager. His face was charming, bewitching, a little insolent, a little wicked. His full soft crimson lips were faintly quivering. The youth smiled as one possessing power—self-confidently and languidly; a magnificent wreath of flowers rested lightly on his shiniug tresses, almost touching his velvety eyebrows. A spotted leopard's skin, pinned up with a golden arrow, hung lightly from his curved shoulder to his rounded thigh. The feathers of his wings were tinged with rose colour; the ends of them were bright red, as though dipped in fresh-spilt scarlet blood. From time to time they quivered rapidly with a sweet silvery sound, the sound of rain in spring.

The other was thin, and his skin yellowish. At every breath his ribs could be seen faintly heaving. His hair was fair, thin, and straight; his eyes big, round, pale grey . . . his glance uneasy and strangely bright. All his features were sharp; the little half-open mouth, with pointed fish-like teeth; the pinched eagle nose, the projecting chin, covered with whitish down. The parched lips never once smiled.

It was a well-cut face, but terrible and pitiless! (Though the face of the first, the beautiful youth, sweet and lovely as it was, showed no trace of pity either.) About the head of the second youth were twisted a few broken and empty ears of corn, entwined with faded grass-stalks. A coarse grey cloth girt his loins; the wings behind, a dull dark grey colour, moved slowly and menacingly.

The two youths seemed inseparable companions. Each of them leaned upon the other's shoulder. The soft hand of the first lay like a cluster of grapes upon the bony neck of the second; the slender wrist of the second, with its long delicate fingers, coiled like a snake about the girlish bosom of the first.

And I heard a voice. This is what it said: 'Love and Hunger stand before thee—twin brothers, the two foundation-stones of all things living.

'All that lives moves to get food, and feeds to bring forth young.

'Love and Hunger—their aim is one; that life should cease not, the life of the individual and the life of others—the same universal life.'

August 1878.

THE EGOIST

He had every qualification for becoming the scourge of his family.

He was born healthy, was born wealthy, and throughout the whole of his long life, continuing to be wealthy and healthy, he never committed a single sin, never fell into a single error, never once made a slip or a blunder.

He was irreproachably conscientious! . . . And complacent in the sense of his own conscientiousness, he crushed every one with it, his family, his friends and his acquaintances.

His conscientiousness was his capital . . . and he exacted an exorbitant interest for it

His conscientiousness gave him the right to be merciless, and to do no good deeds beyond what it dictated to him; and he was merciless, and did no good . . . for good that is dictated is no good at all.

He took no interest in any one except his own exemplary self, and was genuinely indignant if others did not take as studious an interest in it!

At the same time he did not consider himself an egoist, and was particularly severe in censuring, and keen in detecting egoists and egoism.

To be sure he was. The egoism of another was a check on his own.

Not recognising the smallest weakness in himself he did not understand, did not tolerate any weakness in any one. He did not, in fact, understand any one or any thing, since he was all, on all sides, above and below, before and behind, encircled by himself.

He did not even understand the meaning of forgiveness. He had never had to forgive himself. . . . What inducement could he have to forgive others?

Before the tribunal of his own conscience, before the face of his own God, he, this marvel, this monster of virtue, raised his eyes heavenwards, and with clear unfaltering voice declared, 'Yes, I am an exemplary, a truly moral man!'

He will repeat these words on his deathbed, and there will be no throb even then in his heart of stone—in that heart without stain or blemish!

Oh, hideousness of self-complacent, unbending, cheaply bought virtue; thou art almost more revolting than the frank hideousness of vice!

Dec. 1876.

THE BANQUET OF THE SUPREME
BEING

ONE day the Supreme Being took it into his
head to give a great banquet in his palace of
azure.

All the virtues were invited. Only the virtues
. . . men he did not ask . . . only ladies.

There were a great many of them, great and
small. The lesser virtues were more agreeable
and genial than the great ones; but they all
appeared in good humour, and chatted amiably
together, as was only becoming for near relations
and friends.

But the Supreme Being noticed two charming
ladies who seemed to be totally unacquainted.

The Host gave one of the ladies his arm and
led her up to the other.

'Beneficence!' he said, indicating the first.

'Gratitude!' he added, indicating the second,

Both the virtues were amazed beyond expression; ever since the world had stood, and
it had been standing a long time, this was the
first time they had met

Dec. 1878.

296

THE SPHINX

YELLOWISH-grey sand, soft at the top, hard, grating below . . . sand without end, where-ever one looks.

And above this sandy desert, above this sea of dead dust, rises the immense head of the Egyptian sphinx.

What would they say, those thick, projecting lips, those immutable, distended, upturned nostrils, and those eyes, those long, half-drowsy, half-watchful eyes under the double arch of the high brows?

Something they would say. They are speaking, truly, but only Œdipus can solve the riddle and comprehend their mute speech.

Stay, but I know those features . . . in them there is nothing Egyptian. White, low brow, prominent cheek-bones, nose short and straight, handsome mouth and white teeth, soft moustache and curly beard, and those wide-set, not large eyes . . . and on the head the cap of hair parted down the middle. . . . But it is thou, Karp, Sidor, Semyon, peasant of Yaroslav, of Ryazan, my countryman, flesh and blood, Russian! Art thou, too, among the sphinxes?

Wouldst thou, too, say somewhat? Yes, and thou, too, art a sphinx.

And thy eyes, those colourless, deep eyes, are speaking too . . . and as mute and enigmatic is their speech.

But where is thy Œdipus?

Alas! it's not enough to don the peasant smock to become thy Œdipus, oh Sphinx of all the Russias!

Dec. 1878.

THE NYMPHS

I STOOD before a chain of beautiful mountains forming a semicircle. A young, green forest covered them from summit to base.

Limpidly blue above them was the southern sky; on the heights the sunbeams rioted; below, half-hidden in the grass, swift brooks were babbling.

And the old fable came to my mind, how in the first century after Christ's birth, a Greek ship was sailing on the Ægean Sea.

The hour was mid-day. . . . It was still weather. And suddenly up aloft, above the pilot's head, some one called distinctly, 'When thou sailest by the island, shout in a loud voice, "Great Pan is dead!"'

The pilot was amazed . . . afraid. But when

the ship passed the island, he obeyed, he called,
'Great Pan is dead!'

And, at once, in response to his shout, all
along the coast (though the island was un-
inhabited), sounded loud sobs, moans, long-
drawn-out, plaintive wailings. 'Dead! dead is
great Pan!' I recalled this story . . . and a
strange thought came to. 'What if I call an
invocation?'

But in the sight of the exultant beauty around
me, I could not think of death, and with all my
might I shouted, 'Great Pan is arisen! arisen!'
And at once, wonder of wonders, in answer to
my call, from all the wide half-circle of green
mountains came peals of joyous laughter, rose
the murmur of glad voices and the clapping
of hands. 'He is arisen! Pan is arisen!'
clamoured fresh young voices. Everything
before me burst into sudden laughter, brighter
than the sun on high, merrier than the brooks
that babbled among the grass. I heard the
hurried thud of light steps, among the green
undergrowth there were gleams of the marble
white of flowing tunics, the living flush of bare
limbs. . . . It was the nymphs, nymphs, dryads,
Bacchantes, hastening from the heights down to
the plain. . . .

All at once they appear at every opening in
the woods. Their curls float about their god-

like heads, their slender hands hold aloft
wreaths and cymbals, and laughter, sparkling,
Olympian laughter, comes leaping, dancing
with them. . . .

Before them moves a goddess. She is taller
and fairer than the rest; a quiver on her shoulder, a bow in her hands, a silvery crescent moon
on her floating tresses. . . .

'Diana, is it thou?'

But suddenly the goddess stopped . . . and
at once all the nymphs following her stopped.
The ringing laughter died away.

I see the face of the hushed goddess overspread
with a deadly pallor; I saw her feet grew rooted
to the ground, her lips parted in unutterable
horror; her eyes grew wide, fixed on the distance . . . What had she seen? What was
she gazing upon?

I turned where she was gazing. . . .

And on the distant sky-line, above the low
strip of fields, gleamed, like a point of fire
the golden cross on the white bell-tower of a
Christian church. . . . That cross the goddess
had caught sight of.

I heard behind me a long, broken sigh, like
the quiver of a broken string, and when I
turned again, no trace was left of the nymphs.
. . . The broad forest was green as before, and
only here and there among the thick network

of branches, were fading gleams of something white; whether the nymphs' white robes, or a mist rising from the valley, I know not.

But how I mourned for those vanished goddesses!

Dec. 1878.

FRIEND AND ENEMY

A PRISONER, condemned to confinement for life, broke out of his prison and took to headlong flight. . . . After him, just on his heels flew his gaolers in pursuit.

He ran with all his might. . . . His pursuers began to be left behind.

But behold, before him was a river with precipitous banks, a narrow, but deep river. . . . And he could not swim!

A thin rotten plank had been thrown across from one bank to the other. The fugitive already had his foot upon it . . . But it so happened that just there beside the river stood his best friend and his bitterest enemy.

His enemy said nothing, he merely folded his arms; but the friend shrieked at the top of his voice: 'Heavens! What are you doing? Madman, think what you're about! Don't you see the plank's utterly rotten? It will break under your weight, and you will inevitably perish!'

'But there is no other way to cross . . . and don't you hear them in pursuit?' groaned the poor wretch in despair, and he stepped on to the plank.

'I won't allow it! . . . No, I won't allow you to rush to destruction!' cried the zealous friend, and he snatched the plank from under the fugitive. The latter instantly fell into the boiling torrent, and was drowned.

The enemy smiled complacently, and walked away; but the friend sat down on the bank, and fell to weeping bitterly over his poor . . . poor friend!

To blame himself for his destruction did not however occur to him . . . not for an instant.

'He would not listen to me! He would not listen!' he murmured dejectedly.

'Though indeed,' he added at last 'He would have had, to be sure, to languish his whole life long in an awful prison! At any rate, he is out of suffering now! He is better off now! Such was bound to be his fate, I suppose!

'And yet I am sorry, from humane feeling!'

And the kind soul continued to sob inconsolably over the fate of his misguided friend.

Dec. 1878.

CHRIST

I SAW myself, in dream, a youth, almost a boy, in a low-pitched wooden church. The slim wax candles gleamed, spots of red, before the old pictures of the saints.

A ring of coloured light encircled each tiny flame. Dark and dim it was in the church. . . . But there stood before me many people. All fair-haired, peasant heads. From time to time they began swaying, falling, rising again, like the ripe ears of wheat, when the wind of summer passes in slow undulation over them.

All at once some man came up from behind and stood beside me.

I did not turn towards him; but at once I felt that this man was Christ.

Emotion, curiosity, awe overmastered me suddenly. I made an effort . . . and looked at my neighbour.

A face like every one's, a face like all men's faces. The eyes looked a little upwards, quietly and intently. The lips closed, but not compressed; the upper lip, as it were, resting on the lower; a small beard parted in two. The

303

hands folded and still. And the clothes on him like every one's.

'What sort of Christ is this?' I thought 'Such an ordinary, ordinary man! It can't be!'

I turned away. But I had hardly turned my eyes away from this ordinary man when I felt again that it really was none other than Christ standing beside me.

Again I made an effort over myself. . . . And again the same face, like all men's faces, the same everyday though unknown features.

And suddenly my heart sank, and I came to myself. Only then I realised that just such a face—a face like all men's faces—is the face of Christ.

Dec. 1878.

II

[1879-1882]

THE STONE

HAVE you seen an old grey stone on the sea-shore, when at high tide, on a sunny day of spring, the living waves break upon it on all sides—break and frolic and caress it—and sprinkle over its sea-mossed head the scattered pearls of sparkling foam?

The stone is still the same stone; but its sullen surface blossoms out into bright colours.

They tell of those far-off days when the molten granite had but begun to harden, and was all aglow with the hues of fire.

Even so of late was my old heart surrounded, broken in upon by a rush of fresh girls' souls . . . and under their caressing touch it flushed with long-faded colours, the traces of burnt-out fires!

The waves have ebbed back . . . but the colours are not yet dull, though a cutting wind is drying them.

May 1879.

THE DOVES

I sTOOD on the top of a sloping hillside; before
me, a gold and silver sea of shifting colour,
stretched the ripe rye.

But no little wavelets ran over that sea; no
stir of wind was in the stifling air; a great
storm was gathering.

Near me the sun still shone with dusky fire;
but beyond the rye, not very far away, a dark-
blue storm-cloud lay, a menacing mass over
full half of the horizon.

All was hushed . . . all things were faint
under the malignant glare of the last sun rays.
No sound, no sight of a bird; even the sparrows
hid themselves. Only somewhere close by,
persistently a great burdock leaf flapped and
whispered.

How strong was the smell of the wormwood
in the hedges! I looked at the dark-blue mass
. . . there was a vague uneasiness at my heart.
'Come then, quickly, quickly!' was my thought,
'flash, golden snake, and roll thunder! move,
hasten, break into floods, evil storm-cloud; cut
short this agony of suspense!'

But the storm-cloud did not move. It lay as

before, a stifling weight upon the hushed earth
. . . and only seemed to swell and darken.

And lo, over its dead dusky-blue, something
darted in smooth, even flight, like a white handkerchief or a handful of snow. It was a white
dove flying from the direction of the village.

It flew, flew on straight . . . and plunged
into the forest. Some instants passed by—still
the same cruel hush . . . But, look! Two
handkerchiefs gleam in the air, two handfuls
of snow are floating back, two white doves
are winging their way homewards with even
flight

And now at last the storm has broken, and
the tumult has begun!

I could hardly get home. The wind howled,
tossing hither and thither in frenzy; before it
scudded low red clouds, torn, it seemed, into
shreds; everything was whirled round in confusion; the lashing rain streamed in furious
torrents down the upright trunks, flashes of
lightning were blinding with greenish light,
sudden peals of thunder boomed like cannon-
shots, the air was full of the smell of sulphur. . . .

But under the overhanging roof, on the sill
of the dormer window, side by side sat two
white doves, the one who flew after his mate,
and the mate he brought back, saved, perhaps,
from destruction.

They sit ruffling up their feathers, and each feels his mate's wing against his wing. . . .

They are happy! And I am happy, seeing them. . . . Though I am alone . . . alone, as always.

May 1879.

TO-MORROW! TO-MORROW!

How empty, dull, and useless is almost every day when it is spent! How few the traces it leaves behind it! How meaningless, how foolish those hours as they coursed by one after another!

And yet it is man's wish to exist; he prizes life, he rests hopes on it, on himself, on the future. . . . Oh, what blessings he looks for from the future!

But why does he imagine that other coming days will not be like this day he has just lived through?

Nay, he does not even imagine it He likes not to think at all, and he does well.

'Ah, to-morrow, to-morrow!' he comforts himself, till 'to-morrow' pitches him into the grave.

Well, and once in the grave, thou hast no choice, thou doest no more thinking.

May 1879.

NATURE

I DREAMED I had come into an immense underground temple with lofty arched roof. It was filled with a sort of underground uniform light.

In the very middle of the temple sat a majestic woman in a flowing robe of green colour. Her head propped on her hand, she seemed buried in deep thought

At once I was aware that this woman was Nature herself; and a thrill of reverent awe sent an instantaneous shiver through my inmost soul.

I approached the sitting figure, and making a respectful bow, 'O common Mother of us all!' I cried, 'of what is thy meditation? Is it of the future destinies of man thou ponderest? or how he may attain the highest possible perfection and happiness?'

The woman slowly turned upon me her dark menacing eyes. Her lips moved, and I heard a ringing voice like the clang of iron.

'I am thinking how to give greater power to the leg-muscles of the flea, that he may more easily escape from his enemies. The balance of attack and defence is broken. . . . It must be restored.'

'What,' I faltered in reply, 'what is it thou art thinking upon? But are not we, men, thy favourite children?'

The woman frowned slightly. 'All creatures are my children,' she pronounced, 'and I care for them alike, and all alike I destroy.'

'But right . . . reason . . . justice . . .' I faltered again.

'Those are men's words,' I heard the iron voice saying. 'I know not right nor wrong. . . . Reason is no law for me—and what is justice? —I have given thee life, I shall take it away and give to others, worms or men . . . I care not. . . . Do thou meanwhile look out for thyself, and hinder me not!'

I would have retorted . . . but the earth uttered a hollow groan and shuddered, and I awoke.

August 1879.

'HANG HIM!'

'It happened in 1803,' began my old acquaintance, 'not long before Austerlitz. The regiment in which I was an officer was quartered in Moravia.

'We had strict orders not to molest or annoy the inhabitants; as it was, they regarded us very dubiously, though we were supposed to be allies.

'I had a servant, formerly a serf of my mother's, Yegor, by name. He was a quiet, honest fellow; I had known him from a child, and treated him as a friend.

'Well, one day, in the house where I was living, I heard screams of abuse, cries, and lamentations; the woman of the house had had two hens stolen, and she laid the theft at my servant's door. He defended himself, called me to witness. . . . "Likely he'd turn thief, he, Yegor Avtamonov!" I assured the woman of Yegor's honesty, but she would not listen to me.

'All at once the thud of horses' hoofs was heard along the street; the commander-in-chief was riding by with his staff. He was riding at a walking pace, a stout, corpulent man, with drooping head, and epaulettes hanging on his breast

'The woman saw him, and rushing before his horse, flung herself on her knees, and, bare-headed and all in disorder, she began loudly complaining of my servant, pointing at him.

'"General!" she screamed; "your Excellency! make an inquiry! help me! save me! this soldier has robbed me!"

'Yegor stood at the door of the house, bolt

upright, his cap in his hand, he even arched his chest and brought his heels together like a sentry, and not a word! Whether he was abashed at all the general's suite halting there in the middle of the street, or stupefied by the calamity facing him, I can't say, but there stood my poor Yegor, blinking and white as chalk!

'The commander-in-chief cast an abstracted and sullen glance at him, growled angrily, "Well?" . . . Yegor stood like a statue, show-ing his teeth as if he were grinning! Looking at him from the side, you'd say the fellow was laughing!

'Then the commander-in-chief jerked out: "Hang him!" spurred his horse, and moved on, first at a walking-pace, then at a quick trot. The whole staff hurried after him; only one adjutant turned round on his saddle and took a passing glance at Yegor.

'To disobey was impossible. . . . Yegor was seized at once and led off to execution.

'Then he broke down altogether, and simply gasped out twice, "Gracious heavens! gracious heavens!" and then in a whisper, "God knows, it wasn't me!"

'Bitterly, bitterly he cried, saying good-bye to me. I was in despair. "Yegor! Yegor!" I cried, "how came it you said nothing to the general?"

'"God knows, it wasn't me!" the poor fellow repeated, sobbing. The woman herself was horrified. She had never expected such a dreadful termination, and she started howling on her own account! She fell to imploring all and each for mercy, swore the hens had been found, that she was ready to clear it all up. . . .

'Of course, all that was no sort of use. Those were war-times, sir! Discipline! The woman sobbed louder and louder.

'Yegor, who had received absolution from the priest, turned to me.

'"Tell her, your honour, not to upset herself. . . . I've forgiven her."'

My acquaintance, as he repeated this, his servant's last words, murmured, 'My poor Yegor, dear fellow, a real saint!' and the tears trickled down his old cheeks.

August 1879.

WHAT SHALL I THINK? . . .

WHAT shall I think when I come to die, if only I am in a condition to think anything then?

Shall I think how little use I have made of

313

my life, how I have slumbered, dozed through it, how little I have known how to enjoy its gifts?

'What? is this death? So soon? Impossible! Why, I have had no time to do anything yet. . . . I have only been making ready to begin!'

Shall I recall the past, and dwell in thought on the few bright moments I have lived through —on precious images and faces?

Will my ill deeds come back to my mind, and will my soul be stung by the burning pain of remorse too late?

Shall I think of what awaits me beyond the grave . . . and in truth does anything await me there?

No. . . . I fancy I shall try not to think, and shall force myself to take interest in some trifle simply to distract my own attention from the menacing darkness, which is black before me.

I once saw a dying man who kept complaining they would not let him have hazel-nuts to munch! . . . and only in the depths of his fast-dimming eyes, something quivered and struggled like the torn wing of a bird wounded to death. . . .

August 1879.

'HOW FAIR, HOW FRESH WERE THE ROSES . . .'

SOMEWHERE, sometime, long, long ago, I read a poem. It was soon forgotten . . . but the first line has stuck in my memory—

'How fair, how fresh were the roses . . .'

Now is winter; the frost has iced over the window-panes; in the dark room burns a solitary candle. I sit huddled up in a corner; and in my head the line keeps echoing and echoing—

'How fair, how fresh were the roses · · ·'

And I see myself before the low window of a Russian country house. The summer evening is slowly melting into night, the warm air is fragrant of mignonette and lime-blossom; and at the window, leaning on her arm, her head bent on her shoulder, sits a young girl, and silently, intently gazes into the sky, as though looking for new stars to come out. What candour, what inspiration in the dreamy eyes, what moving innocence in the parted question-ing lips, how calmly breathes that still-growing,

315

still-untroubled bosom, how pure and tender the profile of the young face! I dare not speak to her; but how dear she is to me, how my heart beats!

'How fair, how fresh were the roses . . .'

But here in the room it gets darker and darker. . . . The candle burns dim and gutters, dancing shadows quiver on the low ceiling, the cruel crunch of the frost is heard outside, and within the dreary murmur of old age. . . .

'How fair, how fresh were the roses . . .'

There rise up before me other images. I hear the merry hubbub of home life in the country. Two flaxen heads, bending close together, look saucily at me with their bright eyes, rosy cheeks shake with suppressed laughter, hands are clasped in warm affection, young kind voices ring one above the other; while a little farther, at the end of the snug room, other hands, young too, fly with unskilled fingers over the keys of the old piano, and the Lanner waltz cannot drown the hissing of the patriarchal samovar . . .

'How fair, how fresh were the roses . . .'

The candle flickers and goes out. . . . Whose is that hoarse and hollow cough? Curled up, my old dog lies, shuddering at my feet, my only companion. . . . I'm cold . . . I'm frozen . . . and all of them are dead . . . dead . . .

'How fair, how fresh were the roses . . .'

Sept. 1879.

ON THE SEA

I WAS going from Hamburg to London in a small steamer. We were two passengers; I and a little female monkey, whom a Hamburg merchant was sending as a present to his English partner.

She was fastened by a light chain to one of the seats on deck, and was moving restlessly and whining in a little plaintive pipe like a bird's.

Every time I passed by her she stretched out her little, black, cold hand, and peeped up at me out of her little mournful, almost human eyes. I took her hand, and she ceased whining and moving restlessly about.

There was a dead calm. The sea stretched on all sides like a motionless sheet of leaden colour. It seemed narrowed and small; a thick fog overhung it, hiding the very mast-tops in cloud, and dazing and wearying the eyes with its soft obscurity. The sun hung, a dull red blur in this obscurity; but before evening it glowed with strange, mysterious, lurid light.

Long, straight folds, like the folds in some heavy silken stuff, passed one after another over the sea from the ship's prow, and broadening as they passed, and wrinkling and widening, were smoothed out again with a shake, and vanished. The foam flew up, churned by the tediously thudding wheels; white as milk, with a faint hiss it broke up into serpentine eddies, and then melted together again arid vanished too, swallowed up by the mist.

Persistent and plaintive as the monkey's whine rang the small bell at the stern.

From time to time a porpoise swam up, and with a sudden roll disappeared below the scarcely ruffled surface.

And the captain, a silent man with a gloomy, sunburnt face, smoked a short pipe and angrily spat into the dull, stagnant sea.

To all my inquiries he responded by a disconnected grumble. I was obliged to turn to my sole companion, the monkey.

I sat down beside her; she ceased whining, and again held out her hand to me.

The clinging fog oppressed us both with its drowsy dampness; and buried in the same unconscious dreaminess, we sat side by side like brother and sister.

I smile now . . . but then I had another feeling.

We are all children of one mother, and I was glad that the poor little beast was soothed and nestled so confidingly up to me, as to a brother.

November 1879.

N. N.

CALMLY and gracefully thou movest along the path of life, tearless and smileless, and scarce a heedless glance of indifferent attention ruffles thy calm.

Thou art good and wise . . . and all things are remote from thee, and of no one hast thou need.

Thou art fair, and no one can say, whether thou prizest thy beauty or not. No sympathy hast thou to give; none dost thou desire.

Thy glance is deep, and no thought is in it; in that clear depth is emptiness.

So in the Elysian field, to the solemn strains of Gluck's melodies, move without grief or bliss the graceful shades.

November 1879.

STAY!

STAY! as I see thee now, abide for ever in my memory!

From thy lips the last inspired note has broken. No light, no flash is in thy eyes; they are dim, weighed down by the load of happiness, of the blissful sense of the beauty, it has been thy glad lot to express—the beauty, groping for which thou hast stretched out thy yearning hands, thy triumphant, exhausted hands!

What is the radiance—purer and higher than the sun's radiance—all about thy limbs, the least fold of thy raiment?

What god's caressing breath has set thy scattered tresses floating?

His kiss burns on thy brow, white now as marble.

This is it, the mystery revealed, the mystery of poesy, of life, of love! This, this is immortality! Other immortality there is none, nor need be. For this instant thou art immortal.

It passes, and once more thou art a grain of dust, a woman, a child. . . . But why need'st thou care! For this instant, thou art above, thou art outside all that is passing, temporary. This thy instant will never end.

Stay! and let me share in thy immortality; shed into my soul the light of thy eternity!

November 1879.

THE MONK

I USED to know a monk, a hermit, a saint. He lived only for the sweetness of prayer; and steeping himself in it, he would stand so long on the cold floor of the church that his legs below the knees grew numb and senseless as blocks of wood. He did not feel them; he stood on and prayed.

I understood him, and perhaps envied him; but let him too understand me and not condemn me; me, for whom his joys are inaccessible.

He has attained to annihilating himself, his hateful *ego*; but I too; it's not from egoism, I pray not.

My *ego*, may be, is even more burdensome and more odious to me, than his to him.

He has found wherein to forget himself . . . but I, too, find the same, though not so continuously.

He does not lie . . . but neither do I lie.

November 1879

WE WILL STILL FIGHT ON

WHAT an insignificant trifle may sometimes transform the whole man!

Full of melancholy thought, I walked one day along the highroad.

My heart was oppressed by a weight of gloomy apprehension; I was overwhelmed by dejection. I raised my head. . . . Before me, between two rows of tall poplars, the road darted like an arrow into the distance.

And across it, across this road, ten paces from me, in the golden light of the dazzling summer sunshine, a whole family of sparrows hopped one after another, hopped saucily, drolly, self-reliantly!

One of them, in particular, skipped along sideways with desperate energy, puffing out his little bosom and chirping impudently, as though to say he was not afraid of any one! A gallant little warrior, really!

And, meanwhile, high overhead in the heavens hovered a hawk, destined, perhaps, to devour that little warrior.

I looked, laughed, shook myself, and the mournful thoughts flew right away: pluck, daring, zeal for life I felt anew.

Let him, too, hover over me, *my* hawk . . .
We will fight on, and damn it all!

November 1879.

PRAYER

WHATEVER a man pray for he prays for a miracle. Every prayer reduces to this: 'Great God, grant that twice two be not four.'

Only such a prayer is a real prayer from person to person. To pray to the Cosmic Spirit, to the Higher Being, to the Kantian, Hegelian, quintessential, formless God is impossible and unthinkable.

But can even a personal, living, imaged God make twice two not be four?

Every believer is bound to answer, *he can*, and is bound to persuade himself of it.

But if reason sets him revolting against this senselessness?

Then Shakespeare comes to his aid: 'There are more things in heaven and earth, Horatio,' etc.

And if they set about confuting him in the name of truth, he has but to repeat the famous question, 'What is truth?'

323

And so, let us drink and be merry, and say our prayers.

July 1881.

THE RUSSIAN TONGUE

In days of doubt, in days of dreary musings on my country's fate, thou alone art my stay and support, mighty, true, free Russian speech! But for thee, how not fall into despair, seeing all that is done at home? But who can think that such a tongue is not the gift of a great people!

June 1882.

THE END

Printed in Great Britain
by Amazon.co.uk, Ltd.,
Marston Gate.